# Night Bloom

A Pepper Rose Cozy Mystery

Book 1

Jess Fischer

Cozied Up Press

Copyright © 2022 by Jess Fischer
All rights reserved.

jessfischerbooks.com

ISBN: 979-8-9860651-0-6 (Paperback Edition)
ISBN: 979-8-986065-1-1-3 (eBook Edition)

Library of Congress Control Number: 2022907104

No part of this publication may be reproduced, stored in a retrieval system, or transmitted in any form or by any means electronic, mechanical, photocopying, recording, or otherwise, without the written permission of the author or publisher.

Cover illustration by: Kaitlynn Jolley

Cozied Up Press
cozieduppress.com

A huge thanks to Wen, Mom and Becky. You guys saw
what I couldn't and helped smooth out those rough edges.

And to Kathie, who once upon a time,
told me I was a writer. Thank you.

*For my Virtuoso.*
*Solid. Uniquely you. A total gift from above.*
*Love you, dude.*

# one

I was eighteen when I took my first call. It went like this:

"9-1-1, what is the nature of your emergency?"

"I had a baby."

"I'm sorry, ma'am. You said you're *having* a baby? Or, you *had* a baby?"

"I had one. While I was sleeping. I just woke up in bed and found it there. And now I don't know what to do."

Being young and unpracticed at world-weariness, I didn't have an appropriate response for this woman. Sure, I've never given birth. But I'm fairly certain I'd know if I did. Thankfully, I kept my big mouth shut and stuck to the script in my three-ringed binder. Mother and child did fine until the ambulance arrived, at which point the instructions told me to end the call. Most people don't think of it, but that's one of the things that makes being a dispatcher incredibly stressful. There is no closure for us. We are the first on the scene. We are the ones bearing the brunt of all the raw emotion. We collect the information, organize the response, and as soon as the help arrives, our job is done. And we never get to hear how the story ends.

Actually, that's not true. Sometimes we do hear how it ends. Right through our headphones. But we won't go there. Suffice it to say, not many 9-1-1 operators make it to retirement on account of the emotional trauma that comes with the job.

So how did I, Pepper Rose, endure to the end? Probably because I was a salty, crusty old maid. Obviously, I didn't start out that way. But my generation did have a different mentality. When I was hired, we didn't have ridiculous things like "self-care tactics" or "emotional resilience training." Back in the day, we showed up for work, did our jobs and went home. Boom. Now they've got the kids all wigged out, looking for signs of PTSD like it's a contagion lurking in the dark recesses of their cubbyholes.

My last day on the job ended just like the first. I walked out of the communications center, squinting at the morning sun as it peeked over the eastern mountains. Working nights was tough, but Mom and I agreed that it helped sustain our compatibility through all the years.

Making that final drive home from work, I started to doubt myself. Maybe I should have worked some relaxation time into my plans, instead of rushing things. Then again, the way everyone was acting, I was probably doing the right thing just ripping off the bandage and getting out of town.

Here's the deal: My (very fraternal) twin sister and I were thirteen years old when Daddy died in a trucking accident. Thankfully, he had an excellent life insurance policy in place, which allowed us to keep the house and continue with few changes. My sister Piper (yes, Pepper and Piper) got married and moved out as soon as we graduated from high school.

I took the dispatching job that same year and stayed in the house with Mom.

Now here's where it gets sticky. Fast-forward thirty years. I'm 48, never been married, never had children, still living in my childhood home in Riverside. Then there's Piper. Still married to her high school sweetheart, living in a ritzy little place in Manhattan Beach, with three grown children all out of the house. With me so far?

It's true, no one asked me to stay behind and take care of Mom. I did it voluntarily. And yes, I did enjoy some financial benefits from the arrangement. However, I do feel like I made some major personal sacrifices for our family over those thirty years, and I don't think it's too much to ask Piper to take her turn. I mean, don't I get a chance to have a life?

When I opened the front door, Mom was standing inside the entry in her jammies, holding a congratulatory foil balloon.

"Aw, Mom," I said. And then I'm not sure what happened. I must have been PMSing, or pre-menopausing, or something awful, because suddenly my throat constricted and I couldn't speak. I fought back the tears with earnest. Because people make really ugly faces when they cry.

As though she were inside my mind, Mom stepped forward and hugged me tight. I hugged her back. In that moment, I felt something inside me unravel. I could sense what it was. For the first time since Daddy died, she was the mother and I was the child. I held onto her and surrendered to myself.

Normally I would never try to talk and cry at the same time, but with my contorted face shielded by my mother's embrace, I let it all hang out. "I hope you don't think I'm trying to get away from you, Mom," I garbled pathetically.

"No, honey. I would never think such a thing."

"Because I'm gonna miss you."

"I'll miss you, too."

"I'll miss all of this. I've never known anyplace else."

"You've worked hard for this, Pepper. You deserve it and I'm happy for you." She pulled us apart and held my shoulders, forcing me to receive her maternal smile. "You have nothing to feel guilty about."

I wiped my nose with my sleeve and blinked away tears. "But I know you're sad. And I know Piper's pissed at me."

Mom squinted her eyes and nodded her head. "And that's okay."

* * *

I fought off sleep until 3 p.m. I thought I'd be able to sack right out, with all the emotional discharge from that morning, but it wasn't so. The rare honest conversation with my mother was reverberating through my head, making it impossible to sleep. It might be too dramatic to call it a "watershed moment," but our exchange that morning gave me a lot to think about. For starters, I was seeing my mom in a whole new light. She was strong. And maybe I had been trying so hard to protect her all this time, that I never saw it. Or worse, never let it manifest.

The other thing was, today was the closest I'd seen her come to taking sides between me and Piper. Granted, she didn't say much; but for her, it was a lot. Giving me permission to pursue my own dreams at the cost of Piper's came as a complete shock. Mom had always been resolved not to show favoritism to either of us. She deserved a reward, honestly, because I don't know how she did it. Me and my sister were complete opposites, which in my opinion would make it humanly impossible for a parent to not gravitate toward one or the other.

Ironically, Mom's staunch diplomacy only served to fuel the rivalry between us. Left to speculate on our own, Piper assumed Mom liked me the best, whereas I always considered her to be the golden child.

I could see it from Piper's point of view. She probably imagined Mom and me sipping tea around the house all day, exchanging the latest gossip about her and her extravagant lifestyle. And I for one wouldn't have balked at the opportunity. However, Mom would have never allowed it.

The way I saw things, Piper had successfully checked all the critical daughter boxes, giving her the victory fair and square. First of all, she managed to leave the house. That was one. Then, she got married and produced grandchildren. That was probably her biggest score. She had never been divorced. Bonus points. Also, she'd managed to keep her figure and her good looks. Although, she'd had some major help in that department. Mom would have been blind not to have noticed.

I didn't hate my sister, but I struggled to keep the bitterness from creeping in. Please consider: if you looked like Roseanne and had Barbie as a twin, you'd be rankled too. Not to mention the whole Barbie Dream House thing. Piper and Scotty lived very comfortably, in a very comfortable neighborhood, with very comfortable friends. It's not that I wasn't happy for their success, but it was hard for me to look at them without seeing two blue collars playing dress-up. It would've been different if they were business professionals, but they weren't. Piper and Scotty owned a towing company, which to me was just one greasy step above organized crime. And that's all I have to say about that.

❀ ❀ ❀

I woke up at midnight, realizing this transition to normal waking hours was going to be a tedious one. I started a pot of coffee and quietly got to work. Most of my things were already packed in the car. Where I was headed, I didn't require much. There was only one item I needed to retrieve from storage.

I entered the garage and flipped on the overhead lights. Our garage had been through several phases over the years. When Daddy was alive, it was primarily dedicated to sheltering the family station wagon. But he was always too cheap to get an electric garage door system, which caused tension between him and Mom. Piper and I used to giggle when Mom came home from the grocery store. She would park the car in the driveway, give the horn a singular blast, and then march indignantly through the front door. She didn't turn off the car, she didn't bring in any grocery bags. She didn't even close the driver's door. Half the time, her purse was left sitting on the passenger seat in broad daylight. My parents never got into any big fights, but they both owned some nasty passive-aggressive skills. Sometimes I miss seeing her with that fire in her eyes.

I located the bin and unsnapped the lid. The first item I spied was the hideous bean and macaroni picture frame I'd made in first grade. Amazingly, I still remember doing that craft. Or at least, I remember getting busted for flicking dry noodles across the room. My school picture was still glued to the center. I looked like such a little nightmare, missing my two front teeth and wearing a stained t-shirt that was too tight on my belly. Not to mention, my short dark curls were still in recovery from Piper's Pretty Pretty Pony Shop. I swear, Mom must have been horrified by the way I looked as a child. Although, I'm still not sure how picture day always seemed to slip by her. The teachers sent notes home ahead of time. Not only that, but Mom actually worked at the school as a lunch lady.

I set my artwork on the ground, careful not to jostle any loose pieces out of place. Next, I came across the chunk of quartz crystal that I'd dug up in the canyon where us kids used to play. Well, I tried to dig it up. The thing was enormous, and not just to my kid eyes. I never did get to see it in its entirety, but I'm guessing it would have weighed at least 10-15 pounds, had it remained intact. Before I could unearth the thing, my dad came looking for me and made me go home for dinner. I returned for my treasure early the next morning, but when I arrived, all I found was a large hole with a few quartz slivers and the dumb little disregarded piece that now sits in my memorabilia box. As best I can figure, the kids from the rival fort must have been spying on me. They probably heard me squealing about my plans to sell the precious stone to a museum at a sizeable cost. The moment I was dragged off to dinner, they must have moved in, hacked up my crystal, and hauled it away. I don't know why I've held on to the thing. It just makes me mad every time I think about it. Those rotten kids are probably all in jail now. Or waking up to find newborns in their beds. Idiots.

I shuffled through old school assignments and pen pal letters, trying to locate the item I was after. Peering into the past could sure stir some emotions. There was comfort, remembering a period of life when the heavy loads were carried by others. There was also confusion and panic, as one pondered the warping of time. And there was another. To me, this was the worst sensation one could experience in life—missing someone you couldn't bring back.

I opened the faded Kodak envelope and pulled out the 5x7. It was a picture of me and my father with our arms draped around each other's shoulders. We were standing in front of our tent at the Bear Springs Campground, where we spent summer vacations. I had just turned thirteen. It was our last time there.

# two

By eight o'clock I was jittery, either from too much caffeine or from the dread of the looming goodbye. But I couldn't leave just yet. I had asked Piper to stop by so we could discuss a few things. Mom and I busted open a pack of cards and brewed some decaf while we waited.

At ten after ten, we heard Piper's Cadillac SUV pull in beside my Corolla. We stopped our game and looked at one another stoically. Without saying anything, we played out my sister's arrival in our heads. First came the high heeled footsteps…there. Followed by the clinking of her gold bracelets…there. And next, she'd push open the door and call out in her raspy voice…

"Ladies, I'm here!"

"In here," I answered. I closed my eyes and took a deep breath—before all the oxygen got sucked out of the room.

Piper strolled in, looking like your everyday mob wife. She had bleached blonde hair, gobs of makeup, and clothes so tight, even a mannequin would have been uncomfortable. She tossed her keys onto the kitchen table and came around to buss Mom and I on the cheek, like we were all girlfriends meeting at some fancy restaurant.

"How was traffic?" I asked—not that I really cared.

"Horrendous," she answered. "And it's even slower moving the other direction. It's going to take me over two hours to get back."

"Well, I'm glad you could make it. It's important we do this," I reminded her. I left my seat and chucked my coffee mug in the sink.

"Let's make it quick," she said. "I'm supposed to be manning the front desk all week. Vinny, our normal office guy, is having to fill in for one our drivers who got beat up pretty bad over the weekend."

"On the job?"

Piper sneered at me. "Of course it was on the job. We don't hire riff-raff."

"Mm-hmm."

"What's that supposed to mean?"

"Nothing."

"C'mon, Pepper. I know you have an opinion. Let's hear it."

"People don't appreciate having their cars stolen and held for ransom, Piper. How's that?"

"What? How dare you? We are enforcers of the law!"

"Ha! Now that's a good one…"

"Girls!" Mom yelled. "That's enough. We have plenty of business to take care of today, so let's get on with it."

I stepped past my sister and cut through the dining room to the door that led into the garage. "Follow me," I said through gritted teeth. "I've got some stuff to show you in here." Mom stayed behind at the table, watching with concern as Piper and I disappeared from her view.

I entered the garage and flipped on a light. "We keep Mom's medical files in this cabinet over here."

"And you're telling me this because…"

"Piper. I'm leaving," I said with frustration. "Don't you get it?" She looked at me blankly, so I went ahead with the explanation. "I know Mom seems fine to you, and she is. For now. But…" I paused and sighed. "Mom has never lived on her own, and I'm not sure we know how independent she really is. She needs a lot of help with things like…her phone. And the remote. And getting on the computer. You know? Things are going to come up, and I'm not going to be there to help her anymore. So…it's you now."

Piper just stared at me, and I swear I saw tears starting to form. It made me want to slug her in the arm.

"We have to face it, Pipe. Mom is at that age where people start losing step with the world. And anything can happen. Someone needs to be here keeping an eye on her, to make sure she's taking her medicine and paying her bills…"

"But I can't come here every day! I have—"

"I know you can't, and I'm not asking you to," I interrupted. "But it would be nice if you could try to visit as often as you can. Especially at first, while she gets used to being on her own. I worry about her getting lonely." Piper was giving me her pouty face. "Look, I plan to call her. It's not all going to land on you. I'll do what I can to help, but you're the one that has to be there for her physically." The conversation came to a standstill, with both of us looking at each other incredulously.

A scratching noise pulled our attention to another door, which led out to the side yard. Piper shot me a worried smile, so I wasted no time in opening the door to see what it was.

"Piper?" I said, feeling my last nerve begin to fray. "Why is there a puppy out here?" I stood in the doorway and watched as a chubby chocolate lab raced around the yard with one of Mom's gardening gloves in his mouth.

"I hope it's okay. I let him through the gate when we got here."

"You never mentioned getting a puppy," I said suspiciously. The little rascal dropped the glove and decided to work the shoe off my foot, instead.

Piper laughed nervously. "He's actually a gift. For Mom." My mouth dropped open. It's my subtle way of inviting someone to *please, go on*. She caught my drift and continued. "Scotty and I thought it was a perfect way to provide her with some companionship."

I was at a loss for words, so I scooped up the runt and carried him into the house. "Look, Mom," I said. "Piper got you a present!" I was thoroughly enjoying myself at this point.

Mom made a "you must be joking" face, followed by a "heads are going to roll" expression. The puppy started to squirm, so I set him onto the linoleum. He skidded into the kitchen and immediately squatted in front of the refrigerator.

Piper's tinted base started to glisten. "We didn't want you to feel lonely, with Pepper leaving you so suddenly." She attempted a smile, then turned her back and tiptoed toward the mess. Piper crouched in her high heels and wiped at the urine puddle with paper towels. "He's had all his shots, he's been neutered," she volunteered cheerfully, as though perfectly unaware of the indignity of it all. "I also brought you a bag of food and some doggie dishes…and a leash! I dropped it all inside the gate."

Mom still hadn't managed to speak, so I stepped in. "And how old is he?"

"Four months. Isn't he a cutey pie?"

I bit my tongue and turned toward Mom, nudging her to answer the question. The look on her face hadn't changed since "heads are gonna roll." Gosh, I hadn't had this much fun since my sister accidentally put the car into drive instead of reverse and nearly drove right through the kitchen on her way to the senior prom.

Piper collected the pile of soiled paper towels and tossed them in the garbage. With her back to us, she scrubbed her hands at the sink while she plotted her exit. "Hey Pepp, I know you need to get on the road. I should probably be heading out as well." She hustled over to the table and snatched her keys. "Mom, I'll be back in a couple days to look in on you." She bent down to give her another kiss on the cheek. "Pepper," she said with a sigh, "I hope you find what you're looking for." We hugged briefly before Piper vamoosed out the front door.

I returned to the table with Mom, who still had not uttered a word. Her silence was becoming unsettling. At last, she looked at me. Her eyes were frosty with anger. "She got a puppy to babysit me? Does she not know that I hate dogs? Have we ever had a dog?" Her volume was increasing with each question. I hadn't seen Mom this angry since Dad was alive.

"I think she…" I started to say.

"She thinks getting her mother a dog will prevent her from having to pay visits!" Mom's hands were twisting together on top of the table. "That girl has always been too caught up in her own affairs to give a crap about our family!" She pounded her fists on the table.

I was shocked into silence. Hearing my mom rant about my sister should have made me feel awesome inside. This was a chance of a lifetime—to gang up on Piper with my mother and unleash forty-eight years of bottled-up tattling? But there was too much emotion going on here. And I knew it wasn't all to do with Piper. Or the dog. It was about me, too. It was about breakfast time and dinner time, and all the changes that were going into effect as soon as I walked out the door.

"Oh, no," I said. "Where's the puppy?" Mom and I bolted from our seats, anticipating the worst. I ran down the hall, checking the bathroom first. I popped my head inside, expecting to find a room filled with shredded toilet paper. But it was empty. I stopped by Mom's room next, fearing for her shoe collection. That, too, was safe. Before I could make my next move, I heard Mom holler, "Found him!"

I followed her voice into my bedroom. We stood shoulder to shoulder and gazed, like visitors peering through the windows of a hospital nursery. There on top of my bed lay the little brown bundle, sleeping snugly, with his head smack-center on my pillow.

Mom tipped her head and gave me a probing sideways glance. "What do you know about that?"

He was so cute and loveable sleeping there, just like a little person. I couldn't take my eyes off him. My heart melted and my voice went child-like. Before I knew what I was saying, I blurted out, "Can I have him?"

Mom wrapped her arm around me. "I don't think you have a choice," she said with a wink. We stood there a few more moments, watching the sweet baby sleep. The idea of bringing a dog along was growing on me by the second. This was going to be perfect. Before I could say anything, Mom validated my thoughts. "What a happy life he's going to have with you."

"Yes, very happy," I repeated in an unconvinced voice, as the tears began to fall. It was time to say goodbye.

"You'll be happy, too," Mom said. "Leaving is always the hard part. But once you two get on the road, that will be behind you. And then only adventure awaits."

"Are you going to be okay?" I asked with a sniff.

"Honey, I'll be great. Change is a part of life. It doesn't always feel good at first, but it's necessary. And wonderful things come from it."

❀ ❀ ❀

Mom was right. As soon as we left the neighborhood, the heaviness in my chest began to lift. We merged onto the freeway, heading north toward Bakersfield.

I made the puppy a bed on the front seat with a folded-up beach towel. But as it turned out, he preferred to ride in my lap, where he had better access to my face. I was so smitten; he could've sat on my head, and I wouldn't have bothered him. We never got to have any pets growing up. This was a whole new thing for me. I could already tell I was going to be a horrible owner.

We had a good six-hour drive ahead of us. It gave me plenty of time to think. And with all the fresh drama, I needed it. As it turned out though, I was thankful for the way things had transpired that morning. Seeing Mom all fired up made me realize that she could handle herself just fine. I was the one making all the fuss, creating problems that didn't exist. Mom didn't need Piper. She probably never even needed me.

Knowing nothing about puppies, I decided we'd better make stops every ninety minutes or so. It was almost time for our first break, so I pulled off at the next Jack-In-The-Box and leashed him up.

"Do you need to do poo-poo? Or pee-pee?" I couldn't believe I was hearing myself talk like this, in this ludicrous baby voice. "Go potty?" Who knew what code words had been used with him in his previous life? I figured I'd stumble onto it eventually. Hopefully Piper hadn't taught him any naughty words while he was under her care.

We walked around a bit, exploring sections of dirt and grass. He didn't seem desperate to go, so I offered him food and water, which he made quick work of. I'd been told that labs like to inhale their food. This was explained to me long ago by a kid down the street, whose parents were kind enough to compare my eating habits to their deceased dog while having me over for dinner one night. I was too naïve then to be embarrassed. But having just witnessed the phenomenon for myself, I was a little horrified.

The good news was that the food in his tummy must have gotten his system going. As soon as he finished eating, his little tail went up and he was sniffing for a place to go. I trailed after him, taking copious notes in my head. When he began to spin in mysterious circles, I stood over him and held the leash up high. Then he crouched and went…big potty. That's what I decided to call it. I could live with that. We did have a problem though. My sister didn't think to include any big potty bags with the new dog starter kit. It took me a few seconds, but I was pretty proud of the solution I came up with. I dug an empty soda cup out of a nearby trash bin, scooped up the mess, and deposited the waste into the receptacle like I was doing a mic drop. Boom. I felt like such a responsible dog owner. If I could have done it without risking spinal cord damage, I might have broken out in the Ickey Shuffle.

Before we left, I scavenged a couple more cups out of another trash can. It was enough to get us to Bakersfield, where I figured we could find a PetSmart.

After we'd been back on the road for a few minutes, my little guy got sleepy and lay down in my lap. I petted him with my non-driving hand and said, "You wanna know where we're goin'?" I paused, giving him time to respond. But he was out cold. "To the most wonderful place on earth. It's got trees and flowers and mountains that go on forever. There are trails to hike, and places to swim—rivers, lakes, even hot springs!" I looked down at my little baby, who was totally unresponsive. But I didn't care. I was feeling so joyful for him, for the magical dog life that he was going to lead, that I just I carried on. "Lots of people visit there, just to experience the beauty for a few days. But me and you, we get to live there. Do you know what a camp host is?" I asked him. "That's our official title. We're kinda like the bosses of the campground, making sure people have a good time and obey the rules. You'll be my sidekick. The camp ranger." I looked down at my perfect chocolate lab—the Gerber Baby of dogs. "Ranger?" I said, feeling it out. My heart swelled, like it was going to burst in my chest. "I love you, Ranger. Thanks for coming with me."

After our shopping spree in Bakersfield, we jumped onto Highway 99 and continued north toward Fresno. This route was literally known as America's Most Dangerous Highway, having logged more fatal accidents per 100 miles than any other roadway in the country. After years of helping people through car crashes, I tended to pay attention to things like this. You wouldn't expect such terrible statistics in a state known for its mild climate, but the weather wasn't to blame for the accidents on this road. It was the age of the road that was the issue. It had no shoulders, tight ramps, and insufficient lighting. Add drunk drivers and speeders, and you had a recipe for disaster.

Being on this road and seeing all the big rigs, I couldn't help but think about my dad. His crash happened on I-5, at the Grapevine. He got caught in a snowstorm and lost his traction on a curve. He was only thirty-six years old. Just a kid, really.

If there was one thing I inherited from my father, it was his romantic escapism. This may come as a surprise, considering the fairly boring life I'd led to this point. But most of the fun of dreaming is just in the imagining. It's looking out the same window every day and building your happy place piece by piece.

My dad talked about his dream all the time. He got the idea when he took a surfing trip to Mexico as a young man. He and a friend stayed in a small beach town, known for its longboarding. Having grown up in Orange Country, Dad was a casual surfer. More than the sport itself, I think he was drawn to the laid-back culture. Anyway, shortly after arriving, they noticed two little boys that were in and out of the water all day long. They rode extremely short boards, probably custom-made. And as my dad would say, those kids were gnarly surfers. He swore neither one was over the age of ten. Their skin was dark, as you would expect, but they had bright yellow hair down to their shoulders.

Daddy was totally enthralled by those little guys. Where did they come from? Who did they belong to? A couple days into their trip, he stopped into a local gift shop. The owner was a Scandinavian man, maybe thirty years old. He told my dad about his family and how they lived. This guy with his wife and two boys, sailed around the world, stopping for a year or two when they found a place they liked. The boys were homeschooled, and his wife made hand-crafted goods, which helped them set up shop whenever they decided to stay on for a while.

Daddy was captivated. Standing in that store, his own fantasy of a nomadic life on the sea was born. I'm sure he spent a lot of his time on the road building on that dream. I know he thought about it, because every time he came home from a long haul, he brought back lottery tickets for us. We got to keep whatever we scratched off, with one exception. If anybody won the jackpot, we were buying a boat and setting sail.

My heart had always been in Bear Springs. It was the only place we ever went for vacations, so it was essentially my home away from home. It was also the place I planned to escape to, in the event of a nuclear holocaust. Daddy taught me a few survival skills over the years. I remember lying in bed as a teenager, imaging myself arriving at Bear Springs, tattered and exhausted. I already knew exactly where I was going to build my shelter—at my favorite campsite. There were several community water pumps around camp, where you could access potable water, so that was already taken care of. The hot springs provided a year-round source of warmth. And foodwise, I knew all the good fishing holes, and the places where you could dive down and find a bunch of lures that had been caught on rocks. It was just sad to think I'd been waiting on an extinction level event to take me back.

That was one of the toughies for me when we lost Daddy, because he was our connection to Bear Springs. I'm sure it never crossed Mom's mind to take us there after he died. I don't think it was her wonderland, or Piper's either. But my father had been camping there since he was a child—and his father before him. In fact, several Rose family photos hung inside the Bear Springs Café—black and whites from as far back as the 1930s, when the Watts family first opened their private campground.

Harvey Watts ran the place now. He and my dad were about the same age, so they had known each other their whole lives and considered themselves close friends. Harvey had a boy named Tim. He was a couple years older than me and my sister. I remember running around with him some.

When I rang Harvey several months earlier to ask about the camp host position, he was thrilled and gave me the job just like that. I also asked if he might consider keeping me on as full-time staff through the winter. I knew they had some folks that stayed behind, even after the camping season was over. And he happily agreed. It meant taking on some other responsibilities, mostly maintenance-type stuff, but I was good for it. I just wanted to be there.

# three

When we reached Fresno, I could feel the tiny pangs of excitement in my stomach. We turned eastward and began our climb up the foothills, into the Sierra Nevada mountains. It would be another two hours until we reached our destination, but to my senses, we were already home.

Bear Springs lay on the outskirts of Yosemite National Park, at roughly 6,000 feet elevation. If you've ever been to Yosemite, you can imagine the scenery at Bear Springs. If not, think mountains, pines, aspens, enormous granite boulders, rivers, grassy meadows, and of course, bears. Today only black bears roam the Sierras, although at one time the massive California Grizzly made its home there as well. The name Yosemite comes from the American Indian Miwok word for grizzly—*uzmati*. In a similar vein, Bear Springs was named to commemorate the native stories about the grizzlies, who enjoyed bathing in the hot mineral springs.

There is only one way in and one way out of Bear Springs. Locals refer to it as "the pass." It's a narrow one-lane dirt road that never stops curving. And it's fifteen miles long, which feels endless when you're only averaging twelve miles an hour. On one side of the road is blasted-out mountainside, and on the other is a deadly cliff.

As a child, I remember complaining of a headache whenever we were on this stretch. Mom finally realized it was because I was always clenching my teeth. But I was right to be worried. Cars that took the corners too fast could not only smash into you head-on, but they could easily plow you off the road. Thankfully, most people knew to drive slowly. Although, even if you did avoid the collision, you still had to get around one another somehow. So that was the other horror—having to drive in reverse until you found a spot wide enough to let the other cars creep past. If I wasn't craning my neck to watch for oncoming cars, then I was twisting it around to make sure Daddy wasn't backing us off the side of the mountain.

Now I moved cautiously, even though I wasn't expecting any traffic. The grounds were still closed for the season, and it was late in the evening, so no one should have been leaving camp. It was killing me though, having to drive this slowly. We were losing daylight and I was dying to see my new home.

A month earlier, I had purchased a thirty-foot camper. It cost me a year's salary, but it was worth every penny. It was gorgeous inside, and more spacious than you'd think. I had it delivered ahead of time. Harvey suggested we do it that way. He orchestrated the whole thing. He had the road closed, showed the delivery guys where to park it, and then he did the entire hook-up himself. The man was amazing.

I maneuvered around the final curve, and the view unfolded before us. It was just how I remembered. Magnificent. I passed the brown and yellow sign announcing our arrival at Bear Springs Campground and continued down the road. We crept toward the sunset, which hovered above in overlapping layers of orange and purple.

"We're home, Ranger," I whispered. He perked up immediately and stood on his hind legs to look out the passenger window.

Heeding the 10 mph signs, we turned in and drove slowly past the general store, where visitors would normally stop to register. The store was closed, so I continued through the parking area, passing the café next. It, too, was empty. Behind the buildings I could see the cabins, where the Watts family and other campground staff were housed. Being the camp host, I would be the only employee that was not in a cabin.

Ranger and I crept along, mesmerized by the rugged beauty. We left the parking area and merged onto the main road once again, following the signs to the campsites. Sensing the end of our journey, Ranger began to whine. As soon as we hit the beginning of the campsite loop, our new home popped into view. It looked like a set for an RV commercial; the scene was so warm and welcoming. Nestled into the camp host nook and framed by silhouetted trees, the camper was all aglow. Every interior and exterior light had been flipped on for us. The window shades had been pulled up, and the two slides were popped out. Even the awning had been stretched out over a picnic table, which was set with a green vinyl tablecloth. In the center sat a vase of flowers and a large, flickering candle. And perched on the bench was my 72-year-old boss, Harvey Watts.

I rolled to a stop and let Ranger jump out my door to his freedom.

"There she is!" Harvey shouted.

"Oh my goodness, Harvey!" I hurried over with arms extended, as he struggled out of the picnic table. "I didn't realize you were waiting for me. I hope you haven't been out here all afternoon." We embraced warmly. "Look at this. It's amazing! You didn't have to go to all this work." I took a few steps back, admiring the set up. Ranger darted about, too excited to know what to explore first.

"I was glad to do it. I've waited a long time for this, Pepper." He paused thoughtfully. "For the day the Rose family returned to Bear Springs."

"Aw. Thank you," I said. "I'm just sorry it took this long."

"Your dad would be happy."

"He would," I nodded.

"You still have those dark curls, just like him," he pointed out. "I always said that you took after Jack, whereas Piper took after your mom."

I chuckled. "There is some truth to that." Ranger tumbled to a halt at my feet. Then he leapt upward, leaving perfect dirt-colored paw prints on my pants. I hoisted him up for an introduction.

"And who is this?" Harvey asked. "I didn't realize you were bringing a partner," he said with a coy smile.

"I hope it's all right. His name is Ranger. He was literally a last-second add-on, thanks to Piper. It's a funny story. I'll have to tell you about it later."

"He'll be a wonderful addition to the family," he said. "Well, it's getting late, and I don't want to keep you from getting settled. How about we meet for breakfast tomorrow, and you can catch me up on everything?"

"Yes, wonderful," I answered.

"You and Ranger mosey over to the café at your leisure, and I'll have Mick prepare some omelets."

"Deal."

He turned to walk up the dirt road. "You know where I am if you need anything. Goodnight, dear."

My exhaustion had temporarily evaporated in all the excitement. There was so much to take in. I climbed the steps and opened the screen door. "Ranger, come and see!" Together we entered our new forever home. I don't know who was more excited. I hoped I didn't piddle on the floor.

Once inside, I could see more of Harvey's handiwork. He'd left surprises all over the place. I explored my new home, shaking my head in amazement. Everything was ready to use. The bathroom had toilet paper and hand towels in place, and my bed had been made with fresh-smelling sheets and blankets. He'd even stocked the kitchen and left a cute Bear Springs magnet on the fridge. I certainly felt welcome.

❀ ❀ ❀

We woke up early, with the sun. I took Ranger outside immediately. The air was cold and crisp, and it smelled deliciously like a campfire. I glanced eastward, in the direction of the main facilities, and saw a thin trail of smoke rising over the trees. I guessed it was Mick the cook, getting his day started.

Although the campground wouldn't be open for another two weeks, the staff were now kicking things into high gear, preparing for the crowds. There would be many trips down the mountain to restock the store and the café pantry. Campsites and bathroom facilities needed to be inspected and repaired. And any new staff, like myself, had to be brought up to speed with the operations of camp.

It seemed too early to bother anyone, so I fed Ranger, threw on a lightweight jacket, and took him out to explore the grounds. We turned down the road and walked around the campsite loop.

Bear Springs was a small campground, with only twenty-five sites available. Each one came with a picnic table, a fire pit, and a bear-proof food locker. There were also several water stations, and bathroom facilities with hot showers.

Coming here as a youngster, I loved the intimacy and remoteness of it all. Because there weren't many other visitors, we usually made friends with the other families. It was great fun, roaming around with a whole gaggle of kids. Nighttime was the best though, playing hide-and-seek in the dark or sneaking off to the hot springs, where we'd soak and tell scary stories. As Ranger and I passed the empty sites, I was able to recall a few of the names and faces from all those years ago. It made me wonder if our shared memories had sustained any of them in the same way they had me.

Rounding the curve, I could hear the sounds of the river growing louder. These were the premier sites back here, the ones along the water. The river seemed to be made for this campground. It was perfectly diverse, having shallow areas where you could cross over the smooth river rocks, and deep pools for fishing and swimming. The rapids were also just tame enough that you could sit in a tube and float down without trepidation.

Having decent places to cross the river was important, as the hot springs were located on the other side, in the marshy meadows. There were several of them, all spread out. You couldn't see them from a distance, but all you had to do to find one was to follow the foot trails that led from one to the other. I still remembered the smell of hot sulfur and the feeling of silky mud between my toes. It made me want to take Ranger right then and there and find a spring to poke my feet into. But I thought better of it, as I wanted to make a decent first impression. Bringing your puppy fresh from a rotten egg mud pit into a restaurant to greet the chef probably wasn't the way to go. Sometimes my own wisdom surprised me.

We continued through the end of the loop. But instead of veering off and returning to our camper, we wandered up the dirt road toward the café and store. I figured it was good to get Ranger familiar with the lay of the land. As we approached the civilized end of camp, I could see lights on in the cafe. Maybe we'd pay a quick visit, I thought.

Ranger bolted ahead of me and ran up the porch steps. The springs on the screen door screeched loudly as I pulled it back. Walking into the rustic dining room, I was delighted to see that nothing had changed inside.

"Hello," I called, as I stepped onto the worn wooden planks. I took a deep breath through my nose and savored the memories. Ranger trotted around the cozy rectangular room with his nose to the floor. Traces of food particles were teasing his senses.

"Hell-o-o," I sang once more. I was starting to make my way toward the back of the café when I heard the slam of the rear screen door. Just briefly, I saw a man pass by the serving window, carrying a large crate. "Mick?"

"Yeah?" came his gruff response. After that bubbly welcome, I was half-expecting a "Who wants to know?"

I invited myself past the counter and into the kitchen, so we could properly meet. Poking my head around the corner, I said, "Hey there, sorry if I startled ya. I'm the new camp host. Pepper."

Mick was in his mid-fifties, tall, with an athletic build. He had light colored eyes and a firm square jaw, covered with white stubble. Scruffy around the edges, but probably cleaned up nice, I imagined. He set the box onto the counter and finally met my eyes. "Oh, yeah. Harvey said you'd be by for breakfast."

I felt my cheeks go hot with embarrassment. "Actually, I was just out on a walk with my dog and saw the lights on. Thought we'd pop in and say hello." Right on cue, Ranger pranced in, looking for attention. "This is Ranger. Ranger, this is Mick."

"Hey, puppy." He squatted like a baseball catcher and let Ranger jump all over him. Despite the sudden barrage of attention, the man remained surprisingly calm. "I used to have a dog here," he said. His large hands enveloped Ranger's head as he petted him playfully.

"You did?" I hated to probe much further, knowing what was coming next. But it would have been equally rude not to ask. "What happened?"

"She died."

"Oh," I said, pretending to be shocked. "That's terrible. I'm sorry to hear that."

"She was fifteen. It was a long time ago." He stood up slowly, while Ranger continued to gnaw on his knuckle.

"You've been working here a while, then?"

"About thirty years."

"No kidding!" I said, this time with genuine surprise. "You must know Bear Springs inside and out. I guess I know who to go to if I have any questions."

"Eh. I keep to the kitchen. Doubt I'd be much help."

Ranger finally released Mick and turned his attention elsewhere. Mick pulled some potatoes from the box and started scrubbing them in the sink. Staring at his back, I got to wondering. First and foremost, is he going to wash his hands properly? Next, I contemplated what would bring a striking young man to a secluded place like this? And then, what has kept him here so long? The questions kept coming one after another, like corn kernels popping in my mind. Does he have family? Do they know where he is? As the silence stretched on, however, it was clear I'd gotten as much as I was going to get out of Mick for the day. The poor guy was probably exhausted from all the jibber-jabber.

I was about to excuse myself, when I heard Ranger welcoming someone at the front of the restaurant. I peeked through the opening. It was Harvey, with perfect timing.

"Morning stranger!" I yelled, as I happily made my way into the dining area.

"Hey! I thought I heard people milling about," he said. "You two get acquainted?"

"We sure did. I was just passing by. Didn't mean to wake everyone up and put them to work so soon." I cackled nervously.

"Never mind that," assured Harvey. "We like to get an early start around here." He proceeded to a table near the window and pulled out a chair. "Have a seat." As I made myself comfortable, he moved to the other end and said, "Mick, ya mind starting a pot of coffee for us?" Harvey took the seat across from me and sat down with a grunt. We smiled at one another, embracing the quiet moment comfortably—one of the few abilities you actually gain with age. I studied his face. He still had the same kind eyes I remembered from long ago.

"How was your first night?" he asked.

"Wonderful. And Harvey, you did not have to go to all that trouble. It must have taken you…"

He shook his head and waved his palms at me. "Don't mention it," he pleaded. "It's just how we do things here. We take care of each other."

Through the service window, I could see Mick's head pop up for a fraction of a second. By the sounds he was making, I gathered he was chopping potatoes. Hopefully home fries—cubed not sliced.

"How is your mother?" Harvey asked.

"Mom's good. Still in the house in Riverside—"

"And she never remarried?"

"Nope," I answered.

"She's going to be lonely, being in that house without anyone else."

I shrugged. "I know. She swears she'll be fine, but…I'm trying to get Piper more involved. Unfortunately, my sister lives in another world. Her idea of helping with Mom was to drop a puppy into the backyard on her way to the office."

Harvey's shoulders bounced with a hearty laugh. "Ranger?"

"Ranger," I answered, rolling my eyes.

"Maybe we can get your mom up here this summer for a visit. Do you think she'd like that?"

"She would love to see you again. That's a wonderful idea."

"*Uph*. I smell coffee. We can serve ourselves." I followed Harvey to the drip pot behind the counter. He filled a thick cream-colored mug and handed it to me.

"I recognize these mugs," I said warmly. "How is it possible that you've managed to keep everything in here the exact same?"

Harvey chuckled proudly as he pulled creamer from a small refrigerator under the counter. "Attention to detail, my dear."

"I mean the tables, the chairs…"

"I have Mick to thank for that. He helps keep this furniture alive with his skillful hands." Harvey turned to give the chef a brief nod. Then he looked out over the lodge-themed dining room and cupped his mug. "My father taught me an important principle before he passed Bear Springs into my care."

"What was that?" I asked.

"People don't like change."

I nodded my head and raised my eyebrows in agreement.

He continued. "You may not know this, but we don't advertise our campground. Never did. Most of the folks that stay at Bear Springs have been coming here year after year, as long as they can remember." He paused and took a sip of his coffee. Then he pointed across the room to the wall where the old photos were still displayed. "We're a part of family tradition. And that is a sacred thing. In a world driven by change, our mission is to keep family traditions alive by providing a place where time stands still."

His profound words resonated inside me. I thought briefly of my father and the life lessons he might have shared, if he'd had the chance. "That's beautiful, Harvey." I approached the wall, where four generations of Roses carried on. Glancing through the old photos, I ignored the one that showed me as a chubby pre-teen wearing short shorts, striped tube socks, and a fluorescent-orange mesh cap with the words KEEP ON TRUCKIN! stitched onto it. Then I stopped. "Here's one I've never seen." I leaned in close toward a black and white photograph, taken on the porch outside the café. "That's my dad as a kid. And my grandparents. Gosh, they're younger than I am…" Harvey stepped in next to me. I continued. "I don't recognize the other family, though."

"That's me, and my mother and father."

"Well, I'll be," I said in astonishment. "Look at that."

"The Roses and the Watts," he said. "We go back to the beginning of Bear Springs. It would have been your great-grandparents that came here originally. They became friends with my grandparents, and the connection never died. For all those years."

"Until Dad passed away."

"Well, yes. Until then."

We stood quietly for a few moments. "Did anyone tell you what happened? Did you know why we just suddenly stopped coming?"

Harvey dropped his head and nodded toward the floor. "My mother got wind of the news, not long after the accident. She was the one that told me. We were devastated. Your dad and I were close, you know." Harvey moved away from the wall and eased himself back into his seat. "Neither of us had siblings. We bonded early on. Couldn't wait to see each other every summer."

"I'll bet," I said, rejoining him at the table.

"When we were teenagers, your dad would come and stay for a month during the summer. He lived with us in the family cabin and helped around camp. We had a blast."

"You're kidding me. I never knew any of this."

"Those were the best days…"

The door opened once again, and two women stepped inside. Harvey turned in his seat. "Hey, the crew is all here," he said. "Mick, why don't you get some plates together for us, and then we can all eat and go over a few things."

We moved to a large round table. Harvey introduced me to Wanda and Nicole, a mother-daughter duo that helped run the store and restaurant. Wanda was a wispy woman, who wore her fortyish years hard. She had the look of a sea-soned casino cocktail waitress who had aged prematurely, due to second-hand smoke and a secret drinking habit. I was no expert, but I felt she could soften her look if she ditched the heavy eyeliner.

Nicole appeared to be nineteen or twenty. She looked like a younger version of her mother, with slim features and big brown eyes. She and Ranger found one another and formed an instant friendship. She picked him up and held him in her lap while we chatted and waited for Mick to join us.

As I learned, this would be Wanda and Nicole's third summer at Bear Springs. Along with Mick, they also lived here year-round. After being at camp for less than a day, I was finding myself more and more impressed by the thought of spending a winter up here. The seclusion felt wonderful when it was only a couple weeks in the summertime with my family, but now, the thought of being semi-trapped in a place like this with just two or three other people... They based horror movies on that kinda stuff.

"Harvey, did the Watts ever winter-over at camp?" I asked, with new curiosity.

"Not to my knowledge. I'm sure my father would've loved to have made his permanent home here, but we always had the flower shops to worry about."

"That's right. Your florist business. Are you still running that?"

"Oh yeah. Have to. Although I'm not so hands-on anymore, thankfully. We've expanded all over the central valley—we're up to eight locations now."

"That's wonderful."

"It is. To be honest though, I'd much rather just have the campground. But...it doesn't generate the revenue." Harvey shook his head. "It wasn't about that for my family, though. We were never here for the money." He smiled weakly, and I could tell he was troubled. He looked around the room, acknowledging each of his staff. "I do wish I could give you all more, though. More than just a place to stay and food to eat." The pain in his eyes was like he was speaking to orphaned children. "It isn't nearly enough—for all that you do." He became misty-eyed and had to clear his throat to continue. "Without you all, Bear Springs would not exist today. My family's dream…our legacy, would have been paved over and covered by hotels and spas by now."

It was uncomfortable seeing the boss becoming emotional in our first meeting. I wasn't sure if I should pat his hand or pass him a tissue…I decided to let the veterans handle the situation, which they did expertly. Mick continued to scrape stubborn potato skins out of a pan, while Wanda stared vacantly at the table, and Nicole whispered sweet nothings to the dog.

A few moments later, Mick exited the kitchen with several plates teetering on his arm, including one that he set on the floor for Ranger. Harvey made a brave recovery and continued as soon as everyone began to eat. "Now, first order of business—has anyone heard from Trevor?" The table was so quiet, I felt like I had mistakenly joined the convent for their silent prayer breakfast. I wished I could offer some sound, but this was the first I was hearing of any Trevor.

Poor Harvey was obviously accustomed to his squad's level of participation. He carried on without a hitch. "I was expecting him three days ago. I've tried his cell a few times, but it goes straight to voicemail."

The eaters kept their heads down. I couldn't take it any longer. "Is this another staff member, Harvey?" I made sure to speak politely and make eye contact, intent on modeling proper social skills.

"Yes, Pepper, he is," Harvey returned, with matching design. We would have these oxygen-starved mouth breathers trained, yet. "He doesn't have an emergency contact listed, so I don't have any other way of reaching him."

I glanced around the table, excited to see this A-team of troubleshooters leap into action. To my complete surprise, someone had an idea.

"You could ask Tim," Mick volunteered between bites.

# four

After breakfast, Harvey invited me to the general store where his office was located, to complete some paperwork. Just like the café, the store hadn't changed a bit. I took inventory as I followed my boss to the back. The historic 30x20 building was now my Walmart Supercenter, so I'd be lying if I said I wasn't dying to know what they had in stock.

"You actually carry dog food here?" I said in amazement.

"You bet," he said over his shoulder. "You'd be shocked by the number of people that forget to pack for Fido. Oh, and I can't remember if I told you this over the phone, but camp employees shop here for free."

"What? Are you serious?"

"It's only right. I can't expect people to pay for soap and shampoo and late-night snacks without any sort of salary."

"Oh, Harvey, that's so sweet. I do get a retirement check every month, though. I'm happy to pay for my personal expenses."

He waved his hand in the air. "I won't hear of it. This is the way we've always done it. Staff members have keys to all the facilities. If you need anything from the store, day or night, you let yourself in and get it. There's a sign-out sheet in my office. Just jot down what you've taken. It helps us keep track of the inventory, so we know what things are being purchased by the guests."

My heart was all aflutter. I never thought I'd top working the little league snack shack. "Aren't you worried about people taking advantage?"

He chuckled. "We don't sell alcohol or cigarettes here, Pepper. If someone wants to OD on Campbell's Chunky, why they can have at it." For a brief moment, I imagined my tiny kitchen cupboard lined with Pringles cans. Harvey unlocked the office and led me inside. "It's all expenses paid here, Pepper. Oh, and there's a request sheet on the clipboard over there. If you need anything that we don't carry in the store, just jot it down and the next time Trevor runs into town…" His voice trailed off. He sighed heavily and stared out the window. "I'm not sure what to do about him," he confessed.

"How long has he worked here?"

"Four years. He only stays for open season, though. He spends the rest of the year living and working at his buddy's car shop. He's a good mechanic—great to have around. And I trusted him to do the job, but…the boy's got no direction. Someone like that, I wouldn't put it past him to just split. I mean, heck. I wasn't paying him. And he got handed all the nasty jobs."

"Oh yeah, what did he do?"

"A bit of everything. He was our floater, helping with anything that needed to be done. He made trips into town for supplies, fixed anything that broke, washed dishes, worked the register in the store… The poor kid never had much down time. We're going to be in a world of hurt without him."

Outside the office window, I spotted Nicole walking up the footpath to the cabins. She appeared to be texting someone on her phone and had a frown on her face. "Why did Mick suggest asking Tim for help in locating Trevor?" I asked. "Was he talking about your son, Tim?"

"Yes," Harvey answered heavily. He settled into the only chair in the room. "I guess I haven't told you about Timothy."

"What is it?" This was sounding juicy. I hung one butt cheek on the corner of his desk. *Don't mind if I do.*

"Tell me what you remember about him," he said.

"Oh gosh. He would have been fifteen or sixteen the last time we were here. I remember my mom telling us about him playing football and having a really bright future. Piper had a big crush on him," I revealed with an impish grin. I almost mentioned the rumor of a near kiss between the two but thought better of it. "He seemed like he was destined for greatness."

"You have an excellent memory," he said glumly.

"What happened?" I asked, jumping ahead.

"He graduated with honors and went on to law school."

I cocked my head, attempting to understand. "Did he drop out?"

"No. He took a position as a public defender."

I was still playing catch-up. "That's the same thing as a lawyer, isn't it?"

"It's an under-paid, over-worked lawyer. Yes."

"But that's okay, right? Surely you aren't caught up in the dollar signs, are you Harvey?"

"Certainly not. Problem is…my son doesn't seem to realize he's not bringing home the same paycheck as his private attorney friends. Timothy is all about appearances. He's got the fancy car, the clothes, the house." Harvey looked genuinely dejected. He shook his head and said, "The boy's gotten himself into terrible debt."

"I see."

Harvey smiled sadly. "Anyhow, Trevor was one of his clients. He was arrested for possession of marijuana. This was just before cannabis was legalized for recreational use. When he got out of jail, he needed a place to land and Timothy knew we were short-handed, so…" I must not have hidden my shock too well, because he continued. "I wouldn't have normally been so quick to hire a guy fresh out of jail but…we'd done it once before and Mick worked out so well that I thought…"

I nodded sympathetically, trying not to judge. It couldn't be easy to find good, reliable workers, given the location and the salary. He continued. "I'll give Timothy a call this morning and see if he has any ideas. If we can't reach Trevor soon, I'm going to have to find a replacement."

"Were Nicole and Trevor close?" I asked on a hunch.

"They hung out a bit together. It was only natural, them being the two youngsters. I don't think there was anything serious between them, though."

I finished filling out the forms. Harvey issued me a set of keys and arranged to meet again in an hour.

Ranger and I left the store and walked to the rear of the building. We joined the path that led up a slight embankment toward the staff housing. The four cabins were set back amongst trees and boulders, with plenty of space and privacy between each one.

We continued along the meandering trail, which eventually wound its way past each home in a circuitous loop. The first place we passed was clearly marked as the Watts Family Cabin. Cabin number two appeared to belong to Mick, judging by the old work boots on the deck. The third cabin looked empty. I presumed it to be Trevor's. As we approached the final residence, I spotted Nicole sitting in the sunlight on the porch steps. She was staring at her phone while sipping a Diet Cherry RC.

Ranger pulled his dirt-covered nose from the ground and spotted his friend. He took off in a clumsy puppy sprint, his body wiggling in every direction. He climbed the steps awkwardly and plunked into her lap. Her serious expression changed immediately, as she couldn't help but laugh. There must be some involuntary nerve impulse that causes the mouth to open wide when you're being licked in the face.

"Howdy," I said, with a friendly wave. "Sure is nice back here."

Nicole responded with a polite but non-committal nod. "Can't ask for a more beautiful place to live, huh?"

Her smile started to fade. "I guess," she responded. I shifted my feet, feeling a flicker of frustration in my chest. I'd made easier conversation with silverfish.

She placed her phone on the step beside her. I gestured toward it and said, "I was shocked to find out we got cell service up here." Nicole reached out and flipped her phone face-down. "I'd been imagining all of us running around camp with walkie-talkies clipped to our belts." That got a little chuckle out of her. "I'm sure it's a lifesaver, being able to keep in touch with your friends from home."

"*Chsst.* Yeah, whatever." That seemed to hit a nerve.

"Do your friends ever drive up to visit you? Seems like a pretty fun place to come and hang out."

"If you're a *cub scout.*" She shook her head and rolled her eyes. "Why do you care, anyway? What's with all the questions?"

"I'm sorry. I wasn't trying to be nosey. I'm just curious to find out what life is like around here, that's all." Ranger hopped off her lap and went sniffing around a large rock.

"It's boring. Does that help?" She shot me a fake smile. I was starting to feel like this girl's mother, with all the snarky looks she was giving me.

"Weird about Trevor, huh?" If this brat thought she was going to run me off with a bit of sass, she had another thing coming. Nicole began to squirm in her seat. I could tell her little trout brain was racing. I pushed on. "You must be pretty worried about him."

She snatched up her phone and soda and quickly jumped to her feet. "Yeah, it'll stink big time if we're down a person all season long." She turned toward the cabin. "I gotta get going."

"I heard you guys were friends."

Over her shoulder she answered, "Hardly." Then she entered the cabin and closed the door with a *bang*.

❀ ❀ ❀

Ranger and I plodded back to the camper to do some more unpacking and organizing. I had just figured out the perfect spot for my Sue Grafton collection, which I faithfully read through once a year, like a synagogue cycling through the books of Moses. I couldn't wait to get the alphabet mystery series in proper order and displayed on the shelf.

Engrossed in my work, the time flew right past me. The next thing I knew, I heard a cute beep outside. I peered out the window to find Harvey waving from his golf cart.

"Got room for two in there?" I asked, pointing to Ranger.

"Of course," he said. "Hop in."

I climbed in and held Ranger in my lap. "Where are we off to?"

"You wanna ruin the big surprise?" he chided playfully.

I squinted my eyes warily and said, "You're going to show me how to clean the bathrooms, aren't you?"

Harvey let out a belly laugh. "Not just that. I'm also teaching you how to turn on the main water and fire up the hot water heaters."

After a thrilling tutorial, Harvey and I did a thorough inspection, making sure the toilets hadn't forgotten how to flush over their long winter break. With business out of the way, we stepped outside and began to chat. "Were you able to reach Tim?" I asked.

"Oh, yes!" he replied. "He said he'd stop by the auto shop on his lunch break. I'm really hoping he can get some answers."

"If you hit a dead end there, you may want to talk to Nicole."

"Oh? Why is that?"

"I have a feeling she knows more than she's letting on. I ran into her a while ago and tried to ask her about Trevor. She got defensive and bolted on me."

"Hmm," he said thoughtfully. I could tell it bothered Harvey to think badly about people. "Hopefully we'll get some good news from Timothy tonight, and we can forget about the whole thing."

"Yeah, hope so," I said. "Hey, you wanna stop by my place and try out the new coffee maker?"

"Love to, my dear."

*　*　*

At the camper, Harvey and I squeezed into my tight dinette. For a moment, I felt like we were two grandparents trying to be good sports in the backyard playhouse. I was glad for the private setting though, because I had been wanting to ask Harvey a personal question. After chatting a few minutes, I said, "I'm sorry to ask, but what happened to your wife? Did she pass away?"

Harvey lowered his mug gently. "Oh, no. Martha is alive and well. She left me long ago—when Timothy was in law school."

"I'm sorry to hear that."

"Thank you. It certainly was a shock. Totally unexpected."

"Another man?"

"Mm-hmm."

I shook my head in disgust. "Her loss."

"I wish it was just her loss," he said sadly.

"What do you mean?"

"The divorce impacted Timothy—quite significantly. And I don't think Martha has a clue, to this day. When she left, his grades started to slip. And I'm pretty sure that's when the heavy drinking and partying started." Harvey swirled the last bit of his coffee and shook his head. "When his mom walked out, the kid lost his way."

"That's terrible. Does he still struggle with substance abuse?"

"I believe so. He lives life in the fast lane. If he's not at work, then he's at a bar with friends, or wining and dining a new girl. And I told you, he's living way outside his means. It's all going to catch up with him someday."

"Sounds like he could use a sabbatical in Bear Springs. Take some time to slow down, detox, reconnect with nature."

"It's a lovely suggestion," Harvey responded. "He would never go for it, though."

"Why not?"

"Bear Springs was never in his blood. I don't know why. He stopped coming up with us as soon as he was old enough to get a summer job."

"That is a shame, Harvey. A real shame." Ranger trotted to the screen door and began to whine. "He may need to go potty. Let me step out with him." I scooted out of the booth and held the door open.

"I should get going, too." Harvey followed me down the steps. "Thanks for the coffee." He lowered himself into his ride and said, "Mick will have some sandwiches for us around noon. And after that, we'll do a little more work around camp." He waved and motored up the path.

I turned to find Ranger, but he was out of sight. This had never happened before, so I panicked a bit. "Ranger? Where'd you go, little buddy?" I looked up and down the road and saw nothing. I ran behind the camper, looking in all directions. Finally, I spotted his rump sticking out from a bush. His tail was thumping wildly. "What did you find, huh?" I made my way over to him as quickly as I could. I was praying he hadn't cornered a skunk. When I reached him, it took me a minute to see what he saw. Perfectly concealed in the brush was a small, speckled fawn.

"Oh my goodness! Did you find a friend? Look how cute!" I stood up straight and looked around, hoping to see the mother. "C'mon, Ranger. We need to leave the baby alone so her mommy will come back and take care of her." I walked back toward the trailer and called for Ranger over my shoulder. But he wasn't budging. Instead, he was hopping around in the downward dog position, trying to get the baby deer to come out and play. I retraced my steps and picked him up. "Nope, we can't do this. I do not need another pet." He whined and wiggled all the way back to the camper. But inside, he refused to settle down. He started scratching at the door. And then the little booger started to bark.

I was in a real pickle. The barking was starting to drive me crazy, and I didn't want him to mark up the door with his claws. At the same time, I couldn't risk him getting between the fawn and its mother. Assuming there was a mother.

A horrible feeling swept over me, as I realized I could end up being responsible for this deer. If it needed care, I was going to have to provide it. This meant bottle feeding. I started to brainstorm. Between the café and the general store, I could find milk, but did the store carry bottles? Not likely. I whipped out my phone and did a search on how to care for abandoned fawns. The first thing I read was to never feed them cow's milk. Great. Goat's milk was an option, but also not likely to be sitting on the shelves of our neighborhood market.

Ranger was now going berserkers at the door. I glanced up and saw why. His spotted friend was right outside, looking at us. She was the cutest thing, standing there like Bambi. I debated what to do. If there's something I've learned over the years, it's that nature knows best. If these two tikes wanted to get together and play, maybe there was no harm in it. I cautiously opened the screen door, hoping I wouldn't regret it, and let him bound down the steps.

I never realized that deer played like dogs. I watched in total amazement as these two creatures bowed to one another and sprung around in circles, in the most joyful-looking dance. I stayed behind in the camper, not wanting to ruin their game. I felt happy for Ranger, having someone to play with. And I was relieved to see that the fawn appeared to be well-nourished and full of energy. It was a good sign that mommy was nearby.

With the phone still in my hand, I turned it to video mode and let it run for three full minutes. Toward the end, the two playmates settled down a bit. They began to sniff one another, as if realizing for the first time that they were different. Then I heard a sound, like a grunting noise. It was coming from the side of the camper, out of my view. The fawn looked up and responded with a mew. Then she trotted off, leaving Ranger standing alone, looking confused. I was shocked when he didn't try to follow. I opened the door and called to him. This time he gladly came. And I knew I had done the right thing.

After lunch, we loaded two golf carts with rakes and shovels. Wanda and Nicole took off in one, while Harvey, Ranger, and I followed in the other. We split up to work on the campsites. With the old fogies on one team, and the ectomorphs on the other, I was beginning to understand the impact that one young male body could make around this place.

I grabbed the rake and began to sweep away the sticks and leaves that had fallen in the off-season, while Harvey shoveled old ashes from the firepit. Ranger was enjoying the work thoroughly, retrieving the sticks I was carefully scattering into the woods. Little stinker. I was just starting to work up a sweat when Harvey's cell phone rang. He pulled it from the pocket of his flannel shirt.

"Did you find him?" I heard him say. He turned his back and began to pace. I could only make out a few grunts and interrogatory mumbles. I considered slowly raking my way toward him, but it was so spy-at-the-cemetery. It made me feel like a sleaze. *Just be patient,* I told myself. *He'll tell me everything.*

I glanced two sites down, where Nicole was looking our way. I wondered if she knew who Harvey was talking to. When he hung up, he immediately started in my direction. From his body language, I could tell the news wasn't encouraging.

"Timothy visited the shop. Talked to the guys. Everyone gave the same story. Trevor left three days ago, saying he was on his way up here. No one has heard from him since."

"Yikes."

Harvey squeezed his forehead and then ran his hand over his bald spot. "He thinks we ought to file a missing person's report."

"Gosh," I replied helpfully. I leaned on my rake and thought for a moment. "Let's have a chat with the ladies. Give them the update and see if Nicole has anything to contribute." We dropped our tools and walked down to campsite number three. The women saw us coming and migrated toward us.

"Just got off the phone with Timothy," Harvey relayed. "Trevor's friends said he packed up and left Fresno three days ago, just like he was supposed to." Wanda and Nicole stood with expressionless faces.

I stepped in. "Have either of you heard from Trevor?" They both shook their heads. "Nicole?" I let her name float in the air before resuming. "It seemed like you were doing a lot of texting this morning for a person that claims not to have any friends."

Nicole squeezed her brows together. She answered defensively, "I never said I didn't have friends. And yes, I tried to reach out to Trevor this morning, but he hasn't answered back."

"Let me know immediately if you do hear anything," Harvey interjected. "I'm going to have to report him missing, otherwise." Nicole's eyes widened with shock. Then she began to fidget with her hair. It was as guilty a look as I'd ever seen.

We worked for two hours, until we'd completed half the sites. Thankfully, Harvey said we could save the rest of the work for the next day. I didn't want to admit it, but I was wiped out. And I was mad at myself for not wearing a hat. My skin hadn't seen the sun for decades.

We piled into the carts and drove to the utility shed, behind the café. As we replaced the equipment, Harvey asked, "How about if we drop by the store after this, and I can show you how we register the guests?"

I was starting to feel shaky, but I was too embarrassed to admit it. "Sure," I replied.

As soon as we entered the store, Ranger made a mad dash down the dog food aisle. "I know where he's going," I said. "Ranger, I already got you a box of biscuits. You can wait until we get home."

"Nonsense. He can have a box here, too. Here you go, boy!" Harvey took a carton of Milk-Bones off the shelf and tossed a treat to Ranger. He caught it in his mouth like a snapping alligator.

I turned to Harvey. "I'm afraid you're going to have to put all the doggie supplies on the top shelf."

He let out a good-natured chuckle. "I don't think any canine on this earth will ever live as good a life as Girl Dog or Ranger."

"Girl Dog?"

"That was Mick's pup. Great little mutt."

I was about to make a snide remark about the name, but I felt a sudden wave of chills run through my body. "Hey, Harv," I said. "I'm really sorry, but…I'm not feeling so great. I think I may have over-exerted myself today."

"Oh no! Let's get you to my office where you can sit down."

"No, I'll be okay. I just need to go home and rest for a bit."

"This is my fault, Pepper. I feel terrible. You haven't acclimated to the altitude. I should have given you a few days before putting you to work like this."

"It's not your fault. I obviously didn't come here in tip top shape…"

"I'll drive you back. You get in bed, and I'll bring you supper in a while. Rest up, get lots of fluids, and you'll be better in the morning."

"That sounds good. But no need to bring me dinner. I'll just grab a can of chili on my way out."

Harvey gave us a lift home. It was frustrating feeling so rotten on such a beautiful day. I knew I needed to lie down, but I didn't feel like shutting myself in just yet. I found my travel hammock in the trunk of my car and strung it in the shade between two trees. Then I got Ranger settled next to me with a doggie bed and a chew toy plugged up with Easy Cheese. Before I lay down, I went inside for a Perrier and my *A is for Alibi*. From here on out, my yearly readings would mark the anniversary of this new chapter of my life. I thought it was fitting.

I must have dozed off while I was reading. When I woke up, I lifted my head to see an empty dog bed. I jumped out of the hammock and fought off a dizzy spell. "Ranger! Ranger!" This was horrible. I did not have the energy to go searching for him. When I bent over to slip on my shoes, my head started to pound. Worst-case scenarios were playing themselves out in my mind. I imagined him being swept down the river or wandering farther and farther into the wilderness. I was working myself into a real nice tizzy when a rustling noise rudely interrupted me. Ranger shot out of nowhere, followed closely by his new best friend, the fawn. My little baby was so proud of himself for arranging this playdate without any help. He ran to me and gave me that loveable Labrador smile that says, "Hi! I'm dumb."

I was so relieved, I didn't care that my skull felt like an ostrich egg in labor. Ranger repeatedly jumped up on my leg, until I reassured him that I was just as happy as he was. The fawn stood fifteen feet away, watching us with interest. "Hello, little one," I said to her. I decided she was a girl. "You need a name, don't you? How about Pearl? Do you like that?"

Even though her speckles would one day fade, I was satisfied with it. "Pearl, you are welcome to play with Ranger anytime you like. As long as it's okay with your mommy, and so long as you don't take Ranger too far away. Deal?"

I heard a twig snap. I looked up to see Pearl's mother slowly exiting the woods in our direction. Ranger and I stood still while she approached her baby. I expected them to get spooked at any moment and dart off together. But instead, as soon as her mother reached her, Pearl nuzzled beneath her and began to nurse. It might have been the sweetest thing I'd ever seen.

Not wanting to disturb the scene, I didn't move a muscle. But Ranger couldn't help himself. He left my side, doing a floppy run over to his friends. I was sure he would chase them away, but neither deer flinched. Pearl continued to suckle while he weaved his way around the mommy's long legs, the way he often did to me. I shook my head in amazement. Ranger certainly had a gift for being welcomed in.

Pearl continued nursing until Ranger's incessant nagging finally caught her attention. They chased each other around a bit more while the two mothers spectated. The wee ones had worked out a cat-and-mouse game, involving a lot of head bobbing and false starting and stopping. Sometimes Pearl would spring straight into the air and buck like a horse. It was spectacular to watch.

The afternoon sun was hanging low, and Pearl's mommy decided it was time for them to move on. She kept a leisurely pace as she retreated into the forest. After a few moments, Pearl followed. To my astonishment, Ranger had this part all figured out. He trotted right back to me. We climbed into the camper and got ready for supper.

# <u>five</u>

By morning, my aches and chills had gone. Having been out of the loop for half a day, I was eager to get back at it. I put on a fresh pair of stretchy jeans and a long-sleeved shirt and checked the clock. It was only seven-thirty. I wasn't sure what to do. It didn't seem like Harvey had any type of schedule in place. Best I could tell, we were just supposed to show up for food and wait to be contacted. Worked for me. I don't know how Mick could stand it though, people randomly trickling in like a chronic post-nasal drip. No wonder cooks were grumpy.

I fed Ranger a half-portion of kibble, certain Mick would serve him up something special. I grabbed a vest and a visor, and we set out. As we hiked up the road, I was feeling muscles I never knew existed. They were sore, but in a good way. Living up here was going to bring about some nice health benefits. I hoped.

I could smell the griddle a long way off. It made me want to quicken my step. *Boy, could I ever get used to this,* I thought. With a lifetime supply of flapjacks and margarine balls on the brain, I was feeling euphoric as I let Ranger and myself into the café. Once inside, however, I stopped short… and the screen door literally smacked my patootie.

"Whoa! Everybody's here," I exclaimed with surprise. The talking stopped abruptly, and all heads turned in my direction. I hated myself for it, but I could feel the beginnings of paranoia creeping in. "This isn't a meeting about me, is it?" I said half-jokingly, just in case it wasn't true.

Harvey laughed and motioned me over. "No, Pepper. Please join us. I'm sorry, I wasn't sure whether to call you. Are you feeling better?"

"Oh yeah," I said, trying to salvage my cool. "I think my body was just tired from switching my schedule and every-thing…" I took an empty seat next to Wanda and noticed a new face across the table. The man wore some sort of uni-form, including a green ball cap, which he had removed and placed on the table in front of him. I was only able to make out a portion of the departmental patch.

"Pepper, this is Stanley. He's our law enforcement con-tact from the Forest Service."

"Nice to meet you," I said. We shook hands across the table. I was surprised by his soft, gentle grip.

"I rang Stan last night and explained the situation about Trevor." At the mention of Trevor's name, my eyes darted straight over to Nicole. She looked like a child who had already asked twice if they could be excused from the table. "Stan contacted Fresno PD for us and got the missing person's report going there. But he's offered to take a look around here as well, to see if anything turns up."

"That's great," I responded.

"In the meantime, I've asked everyone to start thinking about people you know who might be able to help us get through the summer."

"I could check with Piper's boys," I offered. "I think they have jobs already, but maybe they could ask around for us."

"Anything would help," Harvey answered. "We've got two weeks until the campground opens, and plenty of work to accomplish before then."

After everyone had their fill of pancakes and eggs-over-easy, Harvey gave Wanda and Nicole their instructions for the day. Then he invited Stan and me to his office next door. Ranger and I followed behind the man in the army-green slacks and tan polo, as we walked up the path to the store. He was pudgy with a small "p," and slightly knock-kneed. I put him in his early forties. His skin was fair, and he wore his dirty-blonde hair in a military-style haircut. Despite the imposing equipment on his belt, he carried himself with an air of meekness.

We stepped into the store and closed the door behind us. "The office is too cramped," Harvey said. "We can talk privately here." Any lingering insecurities from earlier vanished for good, as I became proudly aware of my inclusion in this top brass meeting. I told myself to keep my lips zipped, though, fearing I might say something truly stupid.

"What did you want to do next, Stanley?" Harvey inquired.

"I'd like to have a look inside Trevor's cabin, if you don't mind, Mr. Watts."

"Sure, let me grab the key."

Harvey retrieved the spare from his office before leading us up the trail to Trevor's place. "I have no idea what we're going to find in there," he warned. "I try to respect people's privacy, as long as they're deserving." We climbed the steps toward the cabin door. "Trevor worked hard and kept his head down. Never had any trouble with him," he said, as he turned the key. He pushed the door open and stepped back, allowing the officer to enter first. Stan found the light switch and gave it a flip, while Harvey pulled up the shades.

I stepped through the door and did a quick sweep of the one-room living space. There was an unmade bed on one end and a tiny kitchenette on the other. In between, there was a small sofa that faced a television on the wall, and a dining table, doubling as a desk. Although a bit rank, the place wasn't completely thrashed, the way I expected. But there was a smattering of trash lying around. Some of this trash caught my eye—namely, the pile of empty soda cans. There were two flavors: Mountain Dew and Diet Cherry RC.

"Be right back," I yelled. I dashed out the door with Ranger on my heels. Even though I was still sore and slightly out of control, the adrenaline had me feeling like Flo-Jo, gliding down the track. That is, until Ranger crossed right in front of me, nearly tripping me. I tell you what. That would have been just perfect. Me limping back to the men with a bloody lip, dirt all over my face, and a hole in my jeans. Suffice it to say, I learned my lesson. I completed the course to Harvey's office at a nice, safe walking pace.

Inside the office, I wasn't sure where to look. But there were only so many places it could be. I slid a drawer out from the filing cabinet and rummaged through the folders. I was starting to doubt myself, wondering if Harvey would even hold on to old records. But then I saw it. This had to be it. I withdrew the file and cackled obnoxiously. Someone had labeled it, "Old Employee Logs." Normally, dangling modifiers enrage me. But I was feeling giddy, knowing I was onto something huge.

I pulled the merchandise sign-out sheet from six months earlier. Then, to be sure, I selected several more logs and screened them as well. The only staff member in recent history to sign-out Diet Cherry RC was Nicole. And just to cross my tees, I verified that Trevor was the sole consumer of the Mountain Dews.

I decided to bring one of the sheets with me, as proof of my brilliant detecting. When Ranger and I returned to the cabin, Stan appeared to be wrapping up his search.

"Find anything?" I asked, trying not to sound out of breath.

"Afraid not. Place is pretty clean." Stan faced me with his hands on his hips, his knees nearly touching.

"What about you?" Harvey asked. "Looks like you turned up something."

"I think so," I said, downplaying my excitement. The men waited for me to continue. "I've had a funny feeling Nicole might be hiding something about Trevor. She gets really nervous whenever we're discussing him, and she denies being friends with him. But look at this." I flipped the paper toward them and pointed to the evidence. "I've gone through several other logs, and she's the only person here that drinks this stuff." The men pulled back and looked at one another. "Judging by all these empty cans, I'd say Nicole and Trevor spent quite a bit of time together."

Harvey looked distressed. "Let's go talk to her," he said with a sigh. We locked the cabin and filed down to the campsites, where Wanda and Nicole were continuing our work from yesterday. Marching toward the confrontation, I was suddenly wishing I didn't have that stupid piece of paper in my hand, which clearly indicated me as the narc. I folded it up and slid it into my back pocket.

As we got closer, Harvey called out to them. "Ladies, would you mind taking a break and joining us at the picnic table, please?" I felt like I was back on the playground, accompanying the yard duty as she rolled up on some delinquent fourth graders.

Mother and daughter seated themselves on one side, while Harvey, Stan, and I worked our way onto the opposite bench.

"Were you able to find somethin'?" asked Wanda. She looked worried and frail.

"No, ma'am, nothing concrete," Stan answered mildly. "Except, well…we believe your daughter may have some information that she needs to share." All eyes shifted to Nicole. Her cheeks turned beet-red. "Nicole, we know you are good friends with Trevor. And we have reason to believe you may know where he is." Nicole kept her mouth closed and avoided eye contact. Her mother also kept her head down. Their postures were not lending them any credit.

I hated to butt in on a police interrogation, but I couldn't help myself. "Nicole, I know you and Trevor texted one another."

"So what? Big deal. I told you I tried to text him yesterday, but he never answered."

"Fine. When was the last time you *did* hear from him— texting or otherwise?" I cocked my head, letting her know she had nowhere to run.

Nicole glanced sideways toward her mother for help. But Wanda's tower didn't put out too many signals, if you know what I mean.

The girl froze, like a chipmunk trapped in the corner of a basement. I sat back and crossed my arms. I knew from all my cop shows to let her sit there in her loaded diaper for a while.

After a good fifteen seconds, Stan broke the silence. "May I look at your text messages?"

"There's nothing on there. I delete all my texts."

Stan took a slow, deep breath. "I want to remind you, Nicole, that this is now an open police investigation. If you are withholding information that could help locate Trevor, it could mean trouble for you."

Nicole put her elbows on the table and cradled her head in her hands. She was close to breaking. I leaned forward to peek at Harvey. His face was filled with worry. He reached across the table and put a hand on her shoulder. "It's all right, honey," he said. "We know you haven't done anything. We just want to make sure Trevor is okay." And with that, Nicole began sobbing into her palms. We would have to wait another minute for her to start talking, but we knew it was coming. In the meantime, I told myself that I was going to have to work on my good cop routine.

I'm not kidding here; but while we waited for Nicole to settle down, Harvey literally whipped a handkerchief out. He passed it to Wanda, who did us all a major solid by slipping it into her daughter's fingers before it was too late.

Nicole's face was red and puffy when it finally materialized, but thanks to Harvey, it was presentable. With the stuffiest sounding nose I'd ever heard in my life she finally said, "He texted be right after he left Fresdo. Said he was goweeg to stop at the lake for sub extra supplies."

"What lake?" Harvey asked.

"I dote doe," she answered. "He didit say."

"What supplies was he getting?"

"I didit ask."

The tension was starting to build again. I was becoming so peeved, I had to stop myself from calling her "Little Missy." "Nicole," I said brusquely. "Why did you not tell us this yesterday?" No answer.

Stan reentered the conversation. "Is it possible that *extra supplies* could refer to drugs?"

She thought for a moment. "I guess it could."

"Did you ever witness Trevor using drugs of any sort?"

"Baybe." She snuffed.

Stan continued. "Did Trevor ever speak about going to Harris Lake to buy drugs?"

Nicole began to squirm. "Possibly. Yeah, I theek so."

Stan clasped his hands together and faced Harvey. "I think we got what we need, Mr. Watts."

Harvey looked like an old paw paw who'd just discovered his granddaughter was a panties model. "Thank you, Stanley. Ladies, thank you for your cooperation. You may return to your work."

Wanda and Nicole jumped swiftly from their bench. But before she scuttled off, Nicole hesitated awkwardly. Then she turned and bent forward to place her dirty hanky on the table in front of Harvey. "Thake you," she said softly.

As the ladies walked away, the three of us stared in horror at the crumpled wad, which was starting to unfold with little sudden jerks.

Not being up on handkerchief etiquette, I remained silent. What is the proper procedure for a soiled, borrowed hanky? Does the damsel take it home and give it a wash before returning it? Or does she assume it is hers now to keep? I pondered this as the men quietly climbed out of their seats.

Being the perfect gentleman, Harvey picked the hand-kerchief up and gently stuffed it into his pants pocket. It nearly made me gag.

❀ ❀ ❀

As we walked back up the road, Stan explained that Harris Lake is a known hotspot for drug activity. He would drive there immediately and have a look around.

When we reached my camper, Harvey said, "Pepper, why don't you take a break. I've got some paperwork to do. We'll meet again for lunch."

"Sounds good," I replied. "Stan, it was nice to meet you. Thanks for all your help." I reached out to shake his hand, but I had lost his attention completely.

"Miss Rose," he said, staring past me. "Are you keeping wildlife at your camp?"

I turned around to see what he was looking at. Over by the hammock, resting in the dog bed, was our fawn.

"What is that?" Harvey asked. He was squinting his eyes to see.

"That's Pearl!" I answered merrily, not realizing how it looked. Harvey and Stan were shocked.

"Miss Rose, it is unlawful to domesticate wild animals. You…"

"No, no!" I assured him. "It's not like that at all. She's not ours. No, she just comes to play with Ranger."

Stan tipped his head to the side. "Is she abandoned?"

"Oh no. Her mother knows. She's totally cool with it."

"You've…talked to her mother?" He was starting to look a little terrified.

Harvey was still trying to bring the deer into focus when Ranger ran over to her. She jumped out of the bed and the two started right where they'd left off the evening before.

"Would you look at that…" Harvey put his hands on his hips and watched them play like it was one of the miracles of life.

Stan remained silent, allowing himself to grow accustomed to the whole ordeal. Then he said, "I must admit, she looks like a healthy, happy mule deer."

"A mule deer?" I echoed.

"They migrate down the mountain each winter and come back up in the spring."

"She and her mom must live nearby," I said. "I'll bet the mom comes back to Bear Springs every year. That's why she's used to being around people."

"That would make sense." Stan reached up and adjusted the bill of his hat. "I guess there's no harm in it—as long as you don't give them any food."

"No food," I repeated. "I don't want any trouble."

Stan's face blushed. He let out a nervous laugh and said sheepishly, "No, Miss Rose. You aren't in any trouble."

"Please, call me Pepper." When our eyes met one another, I felt a funny jump inside. I thought for a moment I was having a heart attack—it nearly scared me to death.

❊ ❊ ❊

After the boys left, I stayed outside with Ranger and Pearl, and gave my mom a call. I caught her up on all the craziness, including me nearly getting arrested by the Forest Service. She thought that was really funny. I offered to text her the video clip of Ranger and Pearl playing together, but she didn't know what that meant. It would have been point-less trying to explain the difference between emailing and texting yet again. Instead, I told her I'd send it to Piper, and they could watch it together the next time she visited.

As soon as we hung up, I sent Piper a quick text, along with the video. I had no idea I was starting a firestorm.

"What the crap is this?" she wrote. "You took Mom's dog?"

Now I was ticked. "I guess this means you haven't been by to see her yet, or even bothered to call…"

"I am a busy person. I don't get to frolic with the deer all day."

"You should be thankful I took the dog. Otherwise, he'd be digging up your yard right now. Mom hates dogs, for the record. If you ever spent time with her, you'd know that." She didn't write back, so I guess I took that round.

# <u>six</u>

Lunch was awkward. After the interrogation session, we were struggling to regain our team spirit. Harvey did his best, making sure we all sat at the big table together. But there wasn't a lot of cross-table chatter going on. Then his cell phone rang. It was Stan, with big news. He had located Trevor's vehicle at the lake. There were no signs of foul play, but no signs of Trevor, either. They were forming a search party.

"I want to go," Nicole cried out. "Please, let me help look for him."

Harvey thought about it, while he had Stan on the line. "Stanley, would it be possible for us to join the search team?"

Stan said they'd be grateful for the extra bodies, and the two hung up.

"You want me to go, too, Harv?" Mick asked. "Or should I stay here and work on dinner?"

"We're all going," the boss answered. "I'll buy us dinner somewhere out." Mick looked excited to have the night off. "We'll all need flashlights and jackets in case it gets late. Let's meet back here in fifteen minutes."

❈ ❈ ❈

The five of us piled into Harvey's over-sized pickup truck. He and Mick took the seats up front, while the three girls sat in back with an excited puppy moving from lap to lap.

Harvey moved incredibly fast along the curvy mountain road. I reassured myself that he could probably drive the pass blindfolded. I had to close my eyes for most of the way though, to keep from getting car sick. Once we hit the main road, it was a quick twenty-five minutes to Harris Lake. As soon as we arrived, we could see emergency vehicles of all shapes and colors. Every nearby agency with a man to spare was lending their help. A few private citizens had volunteered as well.

We hopped out of the truck and joined a crowd of people. Stan was in the center of the huddle, passing out hand-held radios and maps of the area. He explained that this was still a search and rescue, as Trevor could possibly be alive. He also advised that a helicopter would be dispatched to scan the lake, while those on foot searched the surrounding forest.

Since the volunteers were slowly trickling in from all over, they decided to split the search area into small sections, which were all indicated on the map. That way, they could start dispatching groups immediately to each area. Once a group finished their section, they would call in and be assigned to another.

We received our radio and map and set out. Cutting across the parking area, we were stricken by silence. But the mood took an even more somber turn as we passed Trevor's Mazda, filled to the roof with his personal items. In lieu of packing bags, he had thrown his belongings into the backseat in a large heap. Socks, boxer briefs and undershirts lay in the open, for all to see. I tried not to gawk. But as we continued by, I spotted an unopened value pack of Oral-B dental floss, pressed against the rear windshield. It was cool mint. The same exact floss that I used.

Even though I'd never met the boy, I could feel my connection to him growing. And it sent chills down my arms.

When we finally entered the forest, I looked around and felt instant hopelessness. The lake was several miles around. There were hundreds, if not thousands of acres to search. I wondered what in the heck we were out there for. But then I looked around at all those people, most of them total strangers who had dropped everything to try and find this kid. I imagined if it had been me lost out there, how overwhelmed and grateful I would be to each and every person who came to help me. I was suddenly so proud of our little team, and proud to be a part of it. And I realized I had gained a new respect for Nicole, who was the first person to raise her hand.

We searched through the evening, right until dusk. When the daylight was gone, Stan radioed for everyone to return to the parking area. There had been no signs of Trevor. We gathered around and waited to turn in our equipment. Harvey asked Stan what was next. Stan said they would resume the land search in the morning and would also begin dredging the lake. At this news, Nicole began to tremble. I wasn't sure how she would respond, but I slid next to her and pulled her in with one arm. To my surprise, she turned and wrapped both arms around me tight.

❀ ❀ ❀

Harvey offered to drive us to a steakhouse on the other side of the lake. But it was already close to nine o'clock, and we were all exhausted. We opted to get Subway sandwiches from a nearby gas station instead. I'm not sure what it was about that trip to the sub shop, but something happened to me in there. Maybe it was the way Harvey held open the door for us and softly said, "C'mon gang," as he ushered us in. Or it could have been the scooting along in a single file line like we were children again, waiting at the school cafeteria. Or perhaps it was watching these people do something as simple and innocent as naming the vegetables that they wanted on their sandwiches. Whatever the cause, something inside me was moved. After the enormous day we'd just had, to come here and share in an experience so mundane… We were doing the big and small together. Like family.

It was close to midnight when we arrived at camp. Harvey pulled in behind the general store to drop the others off before taking me and Ranger home. Mick must have heard a noise, because as soon as he got out of the truck, he switched on his flashlight and pointed it down the way. Suddenly, he yelled, "Bear!"

Wanda and Nicole shrieked and scrambled back to their seats. The sudden commotion startled poor Ranger from his deep sleep. Mick hopped into his place up front and slammed the door. "Turn on your brights, Harv, and hit the horn." Harvey did so, causing the entire area behind the café to come into view. The dumpster lid was flipped back, and trash was strewn everywhere. And sure enough, the rear end of a black bear could be seen disappearing into the darkness.

"Are there any more?" Wanda whimpered.

"Let's just sit here a moment," Harvey answered. He blasted his horn a few more times.

Mick put his hands on his head and shouted, "Dang it! This is my fault. I didn't lock the dumpster before we left."

"It's all right, Mick," said Harvey. "We were in a hurry to get out of here. There were bigger things to worry about." Harvey put the car into drive and slowly crept toward the mess. He looked in the rear-view mirror toward us ladies and said, "Don't worry. We're perfectly safe in the truck." He came to a stop when we neared the dumpster. His head-lights lit the entire backside of the building, revealing a new problem.

"No, no, no!" Mick shouted. He jumped from the car and ran toward the walk-in refrigerator, whose door was also hanging wide-open.

"Mick, come back!" Harvey shouted after him.

Mick raced to the opening and shone his flashlight into the cold storage room. We watched from the edges of our seats, as his face slowly turned back toward the blinding light with a sad look of defeat.

Harvey exited the vehicle and approached him. He placed his hand on Mick's back, undoubtedly lending him some words of comfort. The boys stood together for a few moments. Then they closed the refrigerator door and set the bolt before returning to the truck.

"Girls, Mick and I are going to escort you home."

"But what about the trash out here?" I asked. "And the fridge? Did they get to all the food in there?"

"They did. I'm afraid nothing's salvageable. But we'll take care of it. Mick and I are going to clean up the trash tonight, and we'll deal with the refrigerator tomorrow."

"I would like to stay and help you guys," I replied.

"So would I," said Wanda and Nicole in chorus.

❊ ❊ ❊

After two weeks, authorities had not uncovered any leads on Trevor, and the recovery operation was called off. The good news was that Harvey had already found a replacement for Trevor. After the bear invasion, he called Tim out of sheer desperation. And Tim delivered once again—this time with a twenty-something named Colt. We cleaned out Trevor's cabin and welcomed our new team member just a few days later.

At first glance, I had my reservations about the guy. Colt was one of those droopy-drawered kids that likes to self-mutilate with ink and piercings. But upon meeting him, I found him to be a surprisingly polite and well-spoken young man—shaved head or not.

The other positive development was that Bear Springs was now officially open, and campsites were starting to fill up. Getting into a routine and staying busy was just what we all needed to get our minds off our missing compatriot.

I was enjoying my new role as camp host immensely. In truth, I was feeling a little guilty though, as it became clear that I had the easiest job out here by far. I told Harvey I'd be glad to help the others anyway I could—filling in at the store or the restaurant, if needed. But he was adamant that the camp host's number one priority is to remain in place as a visible presence—either at my camper, or anywhere around the campsites. He compared me to a friendly beat cop, walking the neighborhood and getting to know the people. This was the best way to keep an eye on things, he assured me. Thankfully, I was still allowed to pop up to the café for meals, though. Cuz things would've turned ugly quick if he'd tried to take that away from me. Would've been like slipping water to a toddler after you've introduced them to Sprite…

❀ ❀ ❀

We sailed through the first three weeks with ease. Nobody tried to light firecrackers, and no one required the first aid kit. Things were nice and quiet. Then one morning, as Ranger and I took our early lap around the loop, he suddenly had a friend beside him. But this time it wasn't Pearl. It was another hound—an Aussie Shepherd. Judging by her body language, she wasn't there to play. She seemed like a sweet dog, but she was panting heavily and had a distinct look of worry on her face that suggested she was lost. And she had no collar.

I wanted her to know we would help, so I kneeled and spoke softly to her. I could see beyond the fear, to the intelligence in her glacier-colored eyes. She remained by my side and allowed me to pet her for a while before we continued walking.

Finding her owners should have been simple. But as we neared the end of the loop, I became worried, because no one recalled seeing this dog around the campground. And neither did I.

We returned to my RV, where I brought her inside for food and water. She drank a ton but was too stressed to eat. Ranger was sure confused. He tried to engage her in play but was forced to quit after she nipped at him several times.

I kept her inside, hoping that with a little rest, she'd settle down and feel better. Eventually she did lie down on the floor, but she couldn't stop panting. A puddle of drool formed beneath her bright pink tongue, which hung from the side of her mouth.

I gave Harvey a call to let him know what we'd found. He reviewed the registration booklet. No one had checked the box to indicate they'd brought a dog with them. He suggested I call the nearest animal shelter to see if anyone had reported a missing Australian Shepherd.

I dialed the number and spoke to a friendly young woman. I explained the situation, but she said no one had called in. She collected the information, however, and created a report on the found dog. She took my phone number and asked if I would be bringing the dog in. I thought for a moment and told her I planned to care for her until we found her owners.

I redialed Harvey and gave him the update. "I was thinking of giving Stan a call. Missing dogs probably aren't a huge priority for the Forest Service, but…it can't hurt. What do you think, Harv?"

Harvey agreed and passed me Stan's work number. As I dialed, my stomach started to feel a bit funny. I told myself it was probably the half-and-half I'd used in my coffee that morning. It had been a touch on the clumpy side, even for my cheap taste. I gripped the phone as it began to ring. My hands were starting to sweat. I hoped I wasn't coming down with a fever.

"Mann speaking," a voice said.

"Is this…Stanley?" I stammered, with a note of surprise.

"It is, who is this?"

A tiny giggle escaped. "It's…Pepper. Rose. From Bear Springs." I could feel a laugh building up. I did my best to hold it in, but it ended up escaping through my nose, like a reverse-snort.

"Pepper, so good to hear from you." Then he paused. "Is something funny?"

"I'm sorry. It's…" And then, without warning, I caught a total case of the inadvertent giggles. It shot out of me like explosive gas. I hadn't had an episode this bad since I was seven, when I got stuck sitting in the pew next to a woman whose singing voice resembled a moaning cow.

Stan waited patiently for my laughter to subside. I apologized as soon as I was able to formulate words. "I am so sorry! I don't know what happened to me there. Something caught my funny bone…"

Stan didn't miss a beat. "Was it my name?"

He caught me red-handed. I felt like such a turd. "It took me by surprise, is all." I started to panic. "You know, surprise is one of the key elements of humor…" Suddenly, I wasn't sure where to put my foot—in my mouth, or in the enormous hole I was digging.

"My parents said they didn't do it on purpose, but…I'm sure you can guess what nickname I've had my entire life."

"Stan the Mann is a great nickname," I assured him. "Better than any of the ones I had growing up."

This seemed to cheer him up a bit. "What did the kids call you?"

"Oh boy. It's a long list: Cracked Pepper, Hot Pepper, Pepper Corn, Whole Pepper Corn, Pimiento, Wilted Rose, Stinky Rose, Rose Hips…"

"Hmm. You might have me beat there," he interjected politely. "Thank you for sharing that."

I chuckled, thankful to have regained a bit of composure. "Anytime. It's my gift to you."

"How kind of you," he answered. I could tell he was smiling. "So, was there a reason for your call?"

"In fact, there was." I was glad he couldn't see me blushing. "I found a lost dog this morning. And she doesn't belong to anyone here. I also checked with the shelter, and nothing turned up there, either. So, I thought I'd let you know, in case you hear of anything. Plus, I hadn't talked to you for a while, so…"

There was a healthy pause before Stan responded. "Oh. I see. Yes…Thank you. I uh, don't know of any missing dogs off hand, but I'll put the word out. I take it the dog is staying with you and Ranger for the time being?"

"Yes, we're going to take care of her. She's a good girl. Seems a bit traumatized, though."

"Well, I appreciate the call. And I'll certainly let you know if I hear of anything."

As soon as we hung up, I grimaced and slapped my forehead with my open palm. What had gotten into me and made me act like such a fool?

I was restless after talking to Stan. But I didn't want to leave our new friend's side, so I decided to give my mom a call. I was surprised by the sound of her voice. It was the first time I'd noticed any hint of sadness. After I told her about the lost dog I said, "How are you doing, Mom? You sound a bit lonely."

"Oh, I don't know. I guess it is a little lonesome around here." Her admission stabbed me in the heart. I wasn't expecting her to fess up so easily.

"Why don't you come up here for a couple weeks? Stay in my camper?"

"Golly, are you sure there'd be room for me? I'd hate to be in the way."

"Are you kidding? I have room to sleep eight people in this thing. And I have an entire outdoor space all set up. We can make a campfire and sit outside playing cards all night. It'll be great! Plus, Harvey keeps bugging me to get you up here. You two would have a blast hanging out together."

"I guess I could think about it."

"What's to think about? Throw some clothes in a bag and drive up!"

"Oh my," she said. "I wouldn't even know what to pack for Bear Springs. It's been so long."

"Right. Well, you'll need the cooler. And your fishing pole and tackle box. Grab the inflatable raft, too. And don't forget your bikini for the hot springs…"

"Pepper…" she growled.

I laughed. "Seriously. You don't need anything special— a couple outfits and a toothbrush. If you need anything that I don't have, trust me—Harvey will go to the ends of the earth to get it for you. The man is an angel."

"Well then," she responded. I could tell she had warmed up to the idea. "I guess I could make some arrangements."

"Great. And listen. Don't tell Piper you're leaving."

"What?"

"Let's just see how long it takes her to notice that you're gone."

"Pepper…"

Our new charge appeared to be feeling better. She had finally calmed down and was breathing normally. I sat beside her on the floor and petted her softly. "Would you like to try some food, honey?" I had already set out a bowl of kibble, but she didn't touch it. I went into the cabinet for a can of wet food and emptied that into a doggie bowl. It was a struggle keeping Ranger away from her grub, but after she sniffed it, she took a timid bite. After another cautious taste, she figured out how hungry she was. I held Ranger back as she licked the bowl clean. "Good girl," I encouraged.

I wasn't sure what to do next. The poor thing couldn't stay cooped up in the camper forever. But I also didn't want her to run away if I let her out. I remembered that I'd bought a larger collar for Ranger to grow into, so I put that on her and leashed her up. I took the dogs out for another lap around the campgrounds, to double check that no one knew her. But the results were the same. We took a quick spin by the store and café as well, with no success.

When we returned to the RV, I tied her to the picnic table with a long rope that I borrowed from Harvey. I brought my laptop outside and made myself comfortable. Before I knew it, our new friend was curled up beside me, fast asleep.

I was working on my fourth straight win in solitaire when a white and green pickup with U.S. Forest Service decals pulled into my slot. Stan hopped out with a cautious smile.

"Stan? What are you doing here? Didn't I just talk to you on the phone?"

A boyish look crossed his face. "Yeah, about three hours ago." He walked over and stood across the table from me. "I received some information and decided to pay you a visit. I almost called..."

"I'm glad you didn't—this is a fun surprise. What's the word?"

"Just after you and I spoke this morning, I took a phone call from a man reporting a missing hiker."

"You're kidding."

"His friend took off yesterday morning on a day hike. Said he was doing the Eagle's Nest trail. That's about ten miles from here, as the crow flies. And it connects to a path that comes right into the back of Bear Springs. Anyway, his friend told him he'd let him know when he got home yesterday afternoon…but he still hasn't checked in."

"That's terrible."

"Yes. I asked if he might have had a dog with him and the caller said that he probably did." Stan moved away from the table and squatted on his heels. "Cinnamon?" he said softly.

The dog's head shot right up, and her ears perked. She whimpered when she first saw Stan crouching a few feet away. Then she rose on all fours and moved toward him. When she reached Stan, she raised up on her hind legs and rested her front paws on his shoulders. Stan hugged her right back. "What a good girl you are, Cinnamon," he said, giving her lots of love.

Of course, Ranger couldn't stand it. He'd been keeping his distance from her. But now that she was being social, he barged right in and interrupted their moment. Cinnamon hopped down and gave Ranger some reluctant attention. There was a clear maturity gap between the two.

"I think she's feeling better," I said. "You seem to have made an impact."

"Ah, well…I'm no animal whisperer," he said modestly. "We did have several dogs when I was growing up, though. I do miss having them around." We watched Ranger and his new pal wrestle in the dirt. She had him pinned on his back in a submissive position. I was glad to see her putting him in his place.

"How about a tour of the camper?" I asked. We left the pups to play outside and climbed up the steps.

Stan removed the hat from his head and stopped inside the doorway. "I'm not going to find a pet racoon in here, am I?"

"Ha. Very funny."

"How is the fawn? Is she still coming around?"

"Pearl is getting big. She and her mom still visit on occasion. They come around on less crowded days. Can I get you something to drink? Coffee? Tea? Bottle of water?"

"Water would be great." I took a cold one out of the fridge and passed it to him. He stood next to me, studying the photo I'd stuck to the refrigerator with the Bear Springs magnet.

"Is that you?"

"Me and my dad. The last time we were here."

"There's a lot of joy in those faces. You two must have had some fun together."

"We did," I said. "This picture was taken just a few months before he died."

"Oh no. I'm sorry."

"Thank you. Bear Springs was our special place. We did a lot of bonding up here."

"Is that why you came back? To be close to your father again?"

"I suppose so," I answered, with a pensive nod. "Anyway, the bedroom and bathroom are down on that end. We've got the couch here that opens up into another guest bed…"

Stan gasped softly. "Is that the entire Sue Grafton collection?"

"It is. You read Sue Grafton?" I tried not to look or sound too shocked. It honestly never occurred to me that she would have a male readership.

"I've read almost all of them. Kinsey Millhone is my favorite fictional character."

I gave him an impressed nod. "Aren't you full of surprises?" I teased.

"Can't judge a book by its cover." He grinned shyly.

"Feel free to borrow them anytime you like."

"If you don't mind—could I take *K is for Killer* home with me?"

"She's all yours."

Stan grabbed the book off the shelf. We had an awkward moment, trying to figure out what to do next. "I really like your place, Pepper. Thanks for showing me around."

"I enjoyed the company. Stop by whenever you like— surprise me again." I couldn't believe myself. I was pretty sure I was flirting.

"There is one more thing," he said. "Would you mind if I took Cinnamon with me? I'm meeting with the rangers, to search for her owner. I thought it might help to bring her along."

"Of course. You can take the rope as well. Or a leash if you prefer. And let me pack some food for her." I gathered a few items and met Stan outside. He untied the rope from the picnic table and led Cinnamon to the truck. As soon as he opened the passenger door, she jumped in and claimed her seat. "I think she's ready to go," I said with a smile.

"I'll call you with any updates."

"Please do. You guys be safe." Ranger and I watched as our friends backed out and left in a cloud of dust. I think we were both feeling sad to see them go.

# seven

At seven o'clock, Ranger and I trekked to the store to see if Harvey wanted to join us for dinner. Wanda was at the register with a customer. She looked up and gave me friendly smile. "Harvey ain't back there, if you're here for him. I think he's in the cabin."

"All right, thank you. How are you doing?" I asked. "Have you had a chance to get dinner yet?"

"Oh yeah. Colt came by and relieved me earlier. I'm all set."

"Good. I'll just grab a few cans of dog food then, before I go." I set off down the aisle.

"Ranger's gettin' so big," Wanda remarked. "Remember how teeny he was when y'all got here? He was like a roly-poly."

"Tell me about it." I dropped a few cans into a plastic bag and returned to the counter. "There's hardly enough room for the two of us on my bed anymore. When I wake up in the morning, I find myself hanging off the edge of the mattress, while he's all splayed out, right in the middle of the darn thing."

Wanda burst into a laugh so sincere, I discovered she was missing a bicuspid.

"Oh! I'd better sign these out." Ranger ran ahead of me and waited outside Harvey's office, where we kept his box of treats. I followed behind and opened the door. "Okay, big boy. Just a couple though, cuz we're on our way to see Mick. You wanna see Mick?" Ranger sat and tilted his head. He knew exactly what going to see Mick meant. I gave him his two biscuits and took a few moments to mark the dog food down on the sign-out sheet.

"Ranger, what do you have?" He was chewing on something, and it wasn't his treat. "What did you get?" I pried his mouth open and pulled out the remnants of a wet, chewed tissue. "Yucky, Ranger." I tossed it into the trash bin, where I noticed several more used tissues. "That's disgusting, buddy. Do not eat dirty Kleenex, please."

We said goodbye to Wanda and trudged up the path to the Watts Cabin. I knocked on the door. "Harv? It's me. You in there?" I heard a muffled reply, which I couldn't quite make out. I cracked the door and made sure it was okay to enter.

"Hi, Pepper. Come on in." Harvey was sitting in a recliner chair next to a lamp. He had a stack of family photo albums on the floor next to him, and one open in his lap. I also noticed a box of Kleenex next to the lamp, and several used tissues lying on the floor near his feet.

"Oh no. Are you all right? You getting sick?"

"No, dear." He chuckled sadly. "I'm afraid you caught me having my annual pity party, is all."

I walked to a loveseat across from him and sat down. "I thought I was the only person that did that," I said with an empathetic smile.

He patted the album. "When I start to feel down, it helps to pull these out. To remember that I'm not doing this alone—I have all these people from the past supporting me."

I frowned. "Are you talking about Bear Springs?"

He dropped his head with a heavy nod. "I'm not a young man anymore."

"Believe me. I don't know how any of you do it. I was thinking about how physically demanding this is on all of you, when I saw Wanda just now. With her having to open and close the store. And Mick, doing the same at the café… It's insane."

"It is a lot."

"Good thing it's seasonal, huh?"

He chortled. "Bear Springs is seasonal. The floral business is not…"

"Oh gosh." I sighed. "You have way too much on your plate, Harvey."

"Thing is, I always managed just fine. I liked keeping busy. But…I guess it's finally starting to catch up with me."

My mind was in problem-solving mode. "What about Tim? Could he start taking over some of your duties?"

Harvey closed the binder and placed it on top of the pile on the floor. "Pepper, even if that boy had any interest in our family businesses…" He trailed off and pulled another tissue from the box. I could literally feel a tightening in my chest, as my heart ached for this man. He dabbed his eyes for a moment, while he gathered a bit of strength. "I'm sorry for unloading on you. I really try not to complain. Especially because, when you get to be my age, you realize that things have a natural way of working themselves out. All that worrying you did your whole life was mostly done in vain. Sometimes I need a reminder, is all."

I sat quietly for a few moments before changing the subject. "I talked to my mom today. She's planning to visit for a couple weeks."

Harvey's face brightened. "Terrific! When is she coming?"

"I'm not sure. But soon, I think."

"I don't want her driving the pass all alone. You tell her I'll arrange to meet her at my house in Fresno. She can leave her car in my garage, and I'll bring her the rest of the way."

"Are you sure? Gosh, that's really nice of you. She is a decent driver, though…"

"Pepper, I won't change my mind. It's done. You just tell me what day she plans to leave."

"I'll call her tonight and let you know."

"This is tremendous news! Just what I needed." Harvey pushed himself from the chair. "Have you eaten dinner yet?"

"In fact, I have not. Shall we?"

"After you, my dear."

❀ ❀ ❀

Harvey, Ranger, and I entered the café and joined the dinner crowd. As always, Harvey acknowledged the guests with kind greetings before we took our seats. Shortly thereafter, Nicole stopped by our table with ice water.

"Good evening, young lady," Harvey said. "Everything going well?"

Nicole smiled. "Uh-huh. It was a pretty easy day, actually."

"Was Colt able to locate the box of receipt paper?"

"Yep, and I showed him how to switch out the empty roll. How about you all? Pepper, were you able to find the owner of that cute dog?"

I couldn't believe this was the same girl I'd met a few weeks ago. Maybe she'd been coming out of a long, boring winter, or perhaps she was just growing up. Hopefully it wasn't the new guy, Colt. I could see a young girl like her falling for his bad boy looks. At any rate, it was nice to see her happy.

"Ah! We've had some developments on that front."

"Oh?" asked Harvey.

"Stan pulled a missing hiker case today. The hiker had told a friend he'd be doing the Eagle's Nest trail, but he never came home. The friend reported it and gave a description of the hiker's dog. It was a perfect match for our girl, so Stan dropped by my place this afternoon to pick her up. Her name is Cinnamon."

"Stan was here today?" Harvey looked surprised.

"He just popped in quickly. He was on his way to search the trail with the rangers and thought Cinnamon might be able to help."

"That was a good idea," Harvey replied. "I hope the gentleman turns up all right." The three of us fell silent for a moment. Images from our search for Trevor played through my head. I knew Harvey and Nicole were thinking about him as well.

"What can I get you two to eat?" Nicole asked. "Mick made his epic beef barley soup today, and there's a bunch left over."

"That will be perfect for me," Harvey answered gratefully. "For you, Pepper?"

"I'll have the same."

"And a small plate for Ranger?" she asked.

"Whatever scraps Mick has saved for him," I replied. Nicole returned to the kitchen with Ranger on her heels. He was in his happy place, with his little rear swaying side to side and his tail pointed straight up. I could hear Mick whispering to him. It made me chuckle.

"Something funny?" Harvey asked.

"Oh, I was just thinking about Ranger. The way he strolls around town, making friends everywhere he goes. I should've named him *Mayor*."

Harvey laughed. "That would have suited him. But I quite like the name you picked."

Just as Nicole came out with our bowls of soup, my cell phone rang. "Oh! It's Stan. I'll take this out back." I answered the phone as I passed through the kitchen. "Hi. How's the search going?"

"We're finishing up here."

"Does that mean you found him?" I exited the building and began to pace in the dirt.

"Yes. Well, most of him." Stan's voice was strained.

I stood still. "He's dead?"

"Yes. He's deceased." Stan sounded tired and emotional. "Looks like a mountain lion attack."

"Oh, Stan, I'm so sorry. I'm sure that was a terrible thing to see." He didn't reply. I imagined a scene too grisly to speak about. Then I started to worry about the dog. "How's Cinnamon doing? Did she see him?"

"We kept her back as soon as we caught sight of the blood. But I think she knows her owner is gone."

"Poor baby. Where is she now?"

"In my truck. I'm finishing up with the rangers, and then I'll head back to the office to work on next of kin notifications. I'm afraid it's going to be a long night."

"You must be exhausted. I wish there were some way I could help. Would you like to bring Cinnamon back here? I'm happy to hold on to her for you."

"I think it's best if I keep her with me. Thanks for all the food and everything, by the way."

"Of course. Hey, listen. I know I can't undo any of what you've been through today. But I just want you to know that I understand how hard it is. I was a dispatcher for the Sheriff's department for thirty years, and…that feeling that's in your gut right now, making you wish you hadn't eaten such a big lunch? Just remember, it'll go away."

There was a pause, while he found his voice. "How come you never told me you were a dispatcher?"

"Gee, let's see… Maybe because every time I've ever seen you, you've been in the middle of a missing person's investigation?"

His tone lightened a bit. "You still could've mentioned it."

"Oh yeah, right. So, when you were turning Trevor's cabin upside down, I should've just rolled in there, flipped open my 9-1-1 operator credentials, and said, 'Thank you, officer, I've got it from here?'"

Stan let out a small laugh. "If I remember correctly, you were the one that discovered our only lead."

"I guess I was. Do I get anything for that, by the way? Maybe a pin-on badge or something?"

He chuckled. "How about a sticker?"

"I'll take a sticker."

"All right, then. I guess I'll have to pay you another house visit sometime."

"I hope no one has to turn up missing for that to happen."

He paused, briefly. "I was thinking maybe, whenever my stomach is ready for another big lunch..."

"I'd love it. And if you have a chance tomorrow, please call and let me know how your notifications went."

"All right," he said. "I appreciate that. It's...nice to know you're there."

"I am here."

"Goodnight, Pepper."

"Night, Stan."

I was lost in my own emotions when I returned to the dining room. Nicole was sitting at our table, drinking a soda. Harvey took one look at my face and assumed we'd had good news. "Peaceful outcome?" he asked.

I realized I'd been caught. "Oh. No, I'm afraid not. No, it was bad news about the hiker, actually. He was killed by a mountain lion." I took my seat, where my bowl of stew was still steaming.

Harvey made a face. "I don't like to hear that."

"Yeah, so disturbing. I could tell Stan was a little shaken up."

"I'd much rather have a bear encounter myself," Harvey said.

Nicole piped in. "It doesn't matter what kind of animal it is; I don't want to become scat of any kind."

"I second that," I said, as I took my first bite. "Mmm, Mick, this soup is amazing." Mick saluted me through the window.

Nicole scooted away from the table. "You need another helping, Harvey?" she asked, as she rose to her feet.

"No, thank you. That soup is so filling. I couldn't eat another bite."

She reached around him to grab his empty bowl. "I'd better start on some dishes."

As soon as she left, Harvey rested his forearms on the table and leaned toward me. "Stan is a nice fellow, Pepper. And he comes from a lovely family."

I was mid-swallow and had to concentrate really hard to not shoot beef barley out of my nose.

"Was I that obvious?" I said, with my hand over my mouth.

Harvey smiled back sweetly. "I promise not to meddle. I just wanted you to know up front that Stan is one of the good guys."

I nodded. "Well, thank you. I appreciate that." My phone started to ring. I pulled it off the table, hoping it was Stan. "Hi, Mom. Getting packed up?"

"I am," she answered. "And I wanted to know, how soon is too soon?"

"Oh." I looked up at Harvey. "Let me ask Harvey—he's sitting right here."

Harvey whispered, "May I speak with her?" He came around the table and took the phone in his hand. "I'll just take this out back," he said softly. Then he disappeared through the kitchen. "Ruth!" I heard him say, as he stepped out the door.

I smiled to myself. Then I pounded the rest of my soup and snuck back to the kitchen for a quick refill. When Harvey returned a couple minutes later, he was glowing like Moses, fresh from the mountaintop. "Looks like you had a nice chat," I said, playfully.

"It was lovely. And we've got everything arranged. I'm picking her up at noon tomorrow." He took his seat and clapped his hands together. The man was bursting with energy. "I think I might like a piece of pie," he said. Then he scooted right back out and trotted behind the counter. He returned with two pieces of boysenberry crumble and a spray can of whipped cream.

Harvey pushed one of the plates in my direction and promptly dug into his pastry. He chewed with pleasure and began to hum "How Great Thou Art." I sat back and crossed my arms, waiting for him to look up. When he did, I tilted my head and raised an eyebrow.

"What is it?" he asked.

"Oh, nothing. I don't like to meddle," I said, with a bratty smirk.

Harvey let my comment slide like a pat of butter from a tall stack of hotcakes. "You'd better eat that soup before it gets cold. My, I've never seen such a slow eater."

I smiled back at him. "A lady must never underestimate the value of healthy digestive practices."

# eight

While I would never want to live in the Middle East, I will admit, they have two things going for them: baklava and public shaming. I was contemplating the latter after I cleaned the camp showers the next morning. I was considering posting a notice with a giant hairball glued to the bottom, which read something like, "To the woman with long, thick, black hair that likes to wipe her loose hairs on the walls of the shower and leave them: KNOCK IT OFF." Then I would sign it with a drawing of a big eyeball.

Time constraints forced me to put that special project aside, however, as I needed to tidy up the camper before Mom's arrival. I was excited about her visit. This would be a great opportunity for her—not only to get out of the smog, but also to return to a place that held such good memories for our family. I wondered if somehow, it might provide her some closure with Daddy.

You'd think thirty-five years would be enough to get over the death of a loved one, but somehow, I think Mom's been treading around the same rut this entire time. I suppose that can happen when someone is taken from you so suddenly and unexpectedly. Like losing a child—the shock just never goes away. Looking back, I guess that is what happened to Mom. After Daddy died, she remained suspended in her grief. She never got another job, never relocated, never dated, never even remodeled the kitchen. Mom simply never moved on.

I was making the spare bed when I heard a car pull up. It was too early for her to be here. I glanced out the window. Stan.

I took a swig of water, hoping to soften my stale coffee breath before I stepped outside. He was holding the passenger door open for Cinnamon when I called out, "Hey, Sheriff. You here to deputize me?" Cinnamon hopped to the ground into Ranger's over-enthusiastic welcome.

"Right," he said, squinting into the sunlight. "Business first." He reached into his back pocket and pulled out a sticker in the shape of a police badge. I was smiling ear to ear as he approached. "Pepper Rose, I hereby deputize thee in the name of the U.S. Forest Service." He gently pulled off the backing and patted it onto my shirt, like a corsage. I bowed my head and curtsied clumsily. Stan burst into a giggle. "I don't think we did that right."

I threw my head back and joined him with a silly laugh. "That was some kind of cross between a baptism and a knighting ceremony!" We looked at one another and laughed some more. Stan's blue eyes were dancing in the sun. When the laughter died down, I gestured toward the picnic table. "What can I get you to drink?"

"I'd love some coffee, if you've got a pot going."

"I do, be right back." I ran inside and filled two mugs. After an extra trip for cream and sugar, I sat across from him. "So," I said in a more serious tone, "how did last night go? Were you able to locate the next of kin?"

"Mm," he said with a nod, as he took his first gulp. "I caught a break. You won't believe it."

"No next of kin?"

"The man was an only child, with no living relatives."

My eyes grew wide with surprise. "You're kidding me."

"It was such a relief." He sipped his drink. "How do you look at someone and tell them their loved one was mauled to death?"

I nodded in agreement. "But what about Cinnamon? I had presumed the family was going to take her."

"That's what I thought, too." We turned to watch the dogs, who were shoving their heads together at the water dish.

"I could talk to Mick. Or even Nicole. One of them would probably love to have her."

"Thank you. But I already found a home for her."

"You did? Who is it?"

"It's me," he said, with a gentle smile.

I gazed back, so pleasantly surprised. "That's wonderful, Stan."

"You should see how smart she is, Pepper. She knows a ton of tricks, and I've already taught her a couple myself. Watch this." Stan climbed out of his seat and stepped back. "Cinnamon," he called. She turned around immediately and sat. "Who is my sweet girl?" Cinnamon raised her right paw in the air. "That's right!" Stan crouched down and opened his arms. Cinnamon ran to him and put her paws on his shoulders, hugging him just as she had done the first time they met. "What a good girl you are," he said, hugging her back. He stood and dug a meaty treat out of his pocket. She gently licked it from his palm.

"You guys are too cute. Honestly. It's like it was meant to be."

Stan blushed and pointed to his hidden stash of treats. "Can I give one to Ranger?"

"Yeah, but don't expect him to do anything for it."

Stan pulled out a nugget and held it in front of Ranger. "Sit," he said. Ranger danced in place. "Ranger, sit." Ranger pranced some more and started to whine. Stan turned toward me in bewilderment. "Pepper. I thought you were kidding. He doesn't even know how to sit?"

I shrugged my shoulders in innocence. "I'm just happy when he pees outside." Stan stood there, shaking his head. "He's still waiting for his treat," I reminded him with a chuckle. "C'mon, don't tease him."

Stan tossed the treat to Ranger, who swallowed it whole. He bent down to pet him. "I talked to my boss this morning about Cinnamon. Told him how intelligent she is. We're going to try to get her certified as a search dog, so she can come to work with me."

"Really?"

"Yep. In fact, she's already been approved to begin some OJT." He stood upright and beamed like a proud dad.

"OJT?"

"On the job training. She had her office orientation this morning, and she's getting a bit of field training now." He crossed his arms. "I think riding in the truck is going to be her favorite part of the job."

"Wow, this sounds amazing!" I shook my head. "I thought Ranger had a cool job. You're gonna make him jealous," I said with a laugh.

Stan returned to the picnic table and extended his hand toward me. "Miss Rose, would you care to join me at the café for lunch?"

My laughter stopped abruptly as I looked at his hand, waiting steadily for mine. "It would be my pleasure." I reached into his grasp, using it as support as I backed out of the bench. "Thank you," I said quietly, barely meeting his eyes when we finally let go of one another. "Shall we take the long way?" I suggested.

Stan had grown quiet. He nodded warmly. It was the first time I'd noticed the laugh lines high on his cheekbones. I liked the way they made his eyes smile.

We turned left, onto the loop. Cinnamon stayed right beside Stan, while young Ranger behaved more like an alley cat, darting ahead to sniff things, then having to sprint to catch up again.

Stan and I strolled comfortably, side by side. Even though the feelings I had inside were foreign and new, nothing had ever felt more natural than walking down that road with him.

"Where'd you grow up?" I asked.

"I'm a native. Our house is two miles from the office. My father was Forest Service as well. I followed in his footsteps."

"That's neat. Are your parents still in the area?"

"Both passed away five years ago."

"I'm sorry."

"They were in their eighties," he said. "My folks were older when they married and had me. Mom was recently divorced, in her early forties. She didn't think she could have children. It was my dad's first marriage, but he had also given up on the thought of becoming a father. Suffice it to say, they

were both ecstatic when they found out they were pregnant."
Stan chuckled. "It's how I got my middle name—Isaac."

"I'm familiar with the reference," I answered, remembering the tale of Abraham and Sarah. "I love it."

"How about you?" he asked. "Where did you grow up?"

"Outside L.A. In Riverside."

"And you mentioned before that your dad died when you were a teen?"

"Uh-huh. It was just me and my mom and sister after that. I have a twin."

"You're kidding! Is she identical?"

"Nope. Put her in a lineup, and she'd be the last one you'd guess was related to me."

"It must have been fun to have a sibling."

"We had our moments," I said. "Anyhow, I became a dispatcher right out of high school. I really wanted to be a police officer, to tell you the truth."

"What stopped you?"

I laughed. "I was terrified of becoming one of the obstacles in the obstacle course."

"Hey, athletics was never my thing, either. In training, the guys called me 'Stan C'mon Mann,' because I was always bringing up the rear on our group runs. I'm sure that if I could do it, you could do it."

"No, Stan. Even if I'd dropped thirty pounds and had gone to the track every day…it would not have ended well. I'm a total klutz. Believe me, I'm the last person you'd want to see running around with a loaded weapon." Two boys rode past us on their dirt bikes. "Anyhow…I got the job as a dispatcher, continued living in my parents' house, and… pretty much led a boring life."

Stan looked my way and smiled empathetically. "That makes two of us then."

"You lived with your folks, too?"

"I did. It only made sense, being so close to work, and in such a rural area. Plus, with them being older, they always needed a little extra help. And then toward the end there…I was their main caretaker."

"Must have been difficult."

"It was a challenge for sure. There was one point where we had two hospital beds in the living room." He shook his head at the memory. "It was the only way we could all be together."

"That's very touching." I imagined him standing between his parents' beds, gently spooning tapioca pudding into their mouths, while old Matlock re-runs played in the background. I could only imagine what Stan must have thought of me, loading up my covered wagon and leaving my elderly mother all alone on the prairie.

"My mom is on her way here right now for a visit."

"Oh really?"

"Yeah. I don't know how long you can stay, but she'll be here in a couple hours. You could meet her."

"I think we could manage that. Cinnamon will learn more out here than she will back at the office."

"Great!" We rounded the corner, and the river came into view. "Have you ever been to the hot springs?"

"I'm ashamed to say it, but no. I haven't."

"Maybe after lunch, I could take you? I mean, it would be pointless to bring Cinnamon all the way to Bear Springs without showing her the main attraction."

"True."

Walking toward us was a father and his son, about five or six years old. They were both carrying fishing poles. "Morning, boys," I called out, as they got a bit closer. "Anything biting?"

The little guy spoke right up. "No. My mommy made us eat breakfast at the café today, so we missed all the good bites."

"Aw, well don't give up," I said, stifling my laughter. "The fish will get hungry again soon." The father gave us a funny grin as he passed by. When they were out of earshot, I said quietly, "I think Mommy's in trouble."

Stan gave me a sideways glance. He mumbled, "Daddy, too, if his son keeps talking like that." Then we erupted into laughter.

I was enjoying our walk so much, I almost didn't want to stop for lunch. Everything was so beautiful outside. It was warm and sunny. The air was clean, the sky was a brilliant blue, and we had all sorts of wildflowers popping up everywhere. It was just the kind of day that makes you happy to be alive.

At the café, a middle-aged couple had just finished and were leaving their tip on the table. The rest of the place was empty. As soon as the couple left, Stan remarked, "Looks like we've got the café all to ourselves."

"Indeed. It works out nicely. Once the late breakfast crowd clears out, it's pretty quiet in here until dinner time. Gives the staff a chance to stop in for a bite when things aren't too hectic."

Nicole popped out of the kitchen with a large salad and a soda. "Hi, Stan," she chirped.

"Hello, Nicole. Nice to see you. How have things been going?"

"Not too bad. Busy, as always."

"I'll bet. Here you go," he said, pulling out a chair for her.

"Oh. Thank you," she said, with an embarrassed smile. She set her food on the table and took her seat.

I motioned for Stan to follow me to the kitchen. When we arrived, Mick was bent over, putting a large pot into the lower cupboard. He stood and turned toward us. His face was red. "Whew," he said. "Head rush." He shook his head and wiped his hands on his apron. "Hey, Stan." Mick extended a hand, and the two guys shook. "Heard about your missing hiker."

"Yes. Sad case."

I jumped in. "Forest Service got a new search dog out of it, though."

"Oh yeah?" Mick asked.

I tipped my head toward the kitchen entrance. We looked through the opening to see Nicole seated at the table, with Ranger and Cinnamon sitting by her side.

"You're keeping the dog? Good for you."

"Yep. In fact, they're getting her certified. Stan's got a partner now." I reached out and patted his back.

Mick's brow furrowed momentarily. He started to walk away. "What can I get you two to eat?"

"Why don't you take a break, Mick? I'll throw something together for Stan and I." I lifted my brows at Stan. "That salad of Nicole's looked pretty tasty. Want a big salad?"

"Sure," he answered.

"There's some leftover chicken breast in the fridge," Mick offered, as he wandered toward the other end of the kitchen.

"Thanks. You want me to make you one, Mick? You look exhausted. Go take a load off and let me serve you for a change."

"I'm all right," he said. "I never sit to eat."

"You know that's not good for you," I nagged, as I made my way to the refrigerator. "You gotta take care of yourself, too."

I glanced over my shoulder and saw Mick hunched over at the sink. "Mick? Are you okay?" My heart raced as I waited for a response. But before he could say anything, he collapsed and fell to the floor in a heap.

"Mick!" I screamed. Panic set in, causing time to slow down. I felt like I was underwater, incapacitated in every way. The world around me became quiet and dim.

The next thing I knew, I was kneeling beside Mick, with Stan at my side.

"Turn him on his back," he said.

And with those simple words, my brain flipped to auto-pilot and thirty years of experience came rushing in. We lay Mick face-up and began our assessment. "Check for breathing and pulse," I said calmly. Stan put two fingers on Mick's neck, while I placed the back of my hand under his nose. Those few seconds felt like an eternity.

"No pulse," Stan said.

"And no breathing," I followed. "Have you done CPR before?"

"Not on a real body," Stan said nervously.

"I'll walk us through." I looked up to see Nicole peering over us with her hands over her mouth and a look of terror on her face. "Nicole, can you hand me a pair of scissors, please?"

"We need some paddles," Stan said. I have an AED in my truck." He began to scramble to his feet.

"Wait, Stan." I grabbed hold of his arm. "Your truck is too far. There's an AED in the office." Nicole located a pair of scissors in a drawer and passed them to me. "Nicole, can you run to Harvey's office? There's an emergency kit in a metal box on the wall, right near the light switch. Bring that to us as quickly as possible."

While she raced after the defibrillator, Stan pulled his radio from his belt and called for help. I snipped at the apron straps around Mick's shoulders and waist. When it finally came loose, I quickly tossed the apron aside.

"Shoot," Stan huffed, after getting no response. "The mountains are blocking the signal."

"Use your cell," I said, keeping my eyes on my task. With scissors still in hand, I was now slicing my way up Mick's white t-shirt, starting from the bottom. I slowed my pace as I neared the collar. When his shirt fell free, I folded each side back, like a medical examiner splaying open the body cavity to get to the organs. As I began CPR, I noticed a faded Semper Fi tattoo above Mick's left pectoral.

I finished a one-minute round on my own before Stan terminated his call. "They're sending a chopper," he advised.

"What's the ETA?"

"Thirty minutes."

"All right. Let me check for breathing and pulse again." I did another quick examination. "Still nothing. Okay. We're going to start two-person CPR." I waited for Stan to settle into position across from me. "Go ahead and do the head-tilt, chin-lift." I watched as he worked. "Good. Now pinch his nose closed, seal his mouth with yours, give him a one-second breath. Perfect. See that chest rise? Now another breath, just the same."

When he was finished, I placed the heel of my left hand between Mick's nipples. Then I covered my left hand with my right, interlaced my fingers, and leaned into the compressions. I counted to fifteen in my head, cautiously conserving my energy. "And two more breaths, please." Stan leaned forward once again, sweat now dripping from his brow. I sat back on my heels and tried to catch my own breath. "That's it. You're doing great, Stan." He finished his breaths and looked at me with worry in his eyes. I began more chest compressions.

We could hear commotion outside. Soon Nicole burst through the front door, with Wanda and Colt following behind her. Their faces reflected horror, as they stared at Mick's half-clothed body, lying lifeless on the floor. Nicole passed me the case. I quickly unzipped it and pulled out the device. I pushed the power button and began to follow the text and voice prompts.

"All right Stan, we're going to peel off the backing and stick each pad exactly where the diagram indicates." Stan and I each placed an adhesive pad on Mick's chest. The automated system began to check Mick's heart rhythm through the defibrillator pads.

Wanda, Nicole, and Colt were huddled together a few feet away. "Is it working?" Wanda asked, with tears dribbling down her cheeks.

"Not yet. The system is still analyzing his heart rhythm. It'll deliver a shock if it's appropriate." I didn't want to tell the whole truth. An AED is useless in the case of a completely stopped heart. Its purpose is only to help reset an abnormal beat. If no electrical activity is found, it will not deliver a shock.

I was holding my breath, praying silently for a miracle. And then it came. A red warning light began to flash, as the computerized voice repeatedly advised us to stand clear. "System charging. Please step back. System charging. Stand clear from the victim." I let my breath out and mumbled a thanks. Stan and I must have gotten something going on our last round of CPR. The flashing red light changed to solid green. "Stand clear from the victim and push the red shock button."

"All right everyone, back up a step. And keep the dogs away." I looked around the room, making sure it was all clear before the electrical shock was delivered. I pushed the button and stood to my feet. The machine let out a sustained beep, and then stopped. Our eyes were glued to the monitor, as we waited for more news.

"Normal heart rhythm restored," the voice said. "Continue to monitor pulse and breathing and wait for emergency personnel."

I dropped back to the floor and checked Mick's pulse for myself. "I can feel it." I placed my cheek near his nostrils. "And he's breathing," I said, looking up at the group. "We got him back."

Wanda broke loose from the group and knelt on the other side of Mick. She took his hand in hers and began to weep. I watched him for a few more moments. He remained unconscious, but his face was filling with color. I stepped away and consulted with Stan. "What time is it?"

He turned his wrist. "One-thirty."

"Harvey and Mom will be here soon. We should give them a call."

"Wait. If Mr. Watts is driving, it might be best to call your mom and let her relay the news."

"Right." I pulled out my phone. With the immediate crisis at bay, my body started experiencing some aftershocks. My hands trembled as I dialed.

"Hi, Pepper. We're almost there!"

"Oh, how much longer?"

She checked with Harvey and replied, "Twenty minutes."

"All right, well, I need you to give Harvey some news. But you need to stay calm because I don't want him to overreact while he's driving."

"Okay," she said cautiously.

"Mick, the cook, has had a heart attack. He's stable now, but still unconscious. We've got a medevac unit on the way. They'll probably get here the same time you do."

She did a good job tempering her reaction. "I see. Hang on, and I'll let him know." She twisted the phone away from her mouth and calmly repeated the message, nearly verbatim.

Harvey kept a level head. I could hear him in the background. "Tell Pepper I hope to be there before the medevac team arrives. But if not, have her find out where they're taking him. And tell her to make sure the hospital has me down as the point of contact."

Mom returned to the phone. "Did you catch that?"

"Yep," I replied. "Got it. You guys drive safely, and we'll see you here soon."

I hung up the phone and nodded some encouragement to the group. "Harvey will be here in twenty minutes. Everything is under control." I squatted down once more to check Mick's vitals, which seemed to be steady. I stood back up. "Hey, Colt, do you mind closing the shop and turning the sign in the café window, please?"

"And Colt?" Stan interjected. "When you're done with that, meet me out front. We need to close off traffic and clear a landing space for the chopper."

"Sure," he answered eagerly. Colt gave his pants a hike and ran out the door.

Nicole, Wanda, and I stayed behind with Mick, keeping a close eye on him. We covered him with a blanket and put a folded kitchen towel beneath his head. Twenty minutes later, I heard the front door open. Harvey and Mom rushed into the kitchen to find us. "Glad you made it," I said, hugging them both. Harvey approached Mick and looked him over, as if trying to think of some way to help. "He's doing all right," I assured him. "Help will be here any minute." Harvey was speechless. He stared down at the man who had been under his wing for thirty years. There was no telling what they'd been through together in that length of time.

"Are you going to contact his family?" I asked.

Harvey kept his eyes on Mick and shook his head. "Mick has never made any mention of family."

"And you never asked," I said, letting my emotions get the best of me. I have always been mystified by the communication style of men.

"No, I didn't. The best way to get a man to open up, is to give him some space. If he has something to share, he'll do it. When he's ready."

My remark had clearly irritated him right back. I took a deep breath and let it go.

"I'm wondering if I should go to the hospital," Harvey said. "Someone should be with him, shouldn't they?"

"I don't know, Harv. I'm not sure how much you'll be able to do there. He'll probably be in intensive care for at least a couple days. Only family will be allowed to visit… Plus, we're down a man, once again. What are we going to do without a cook?"

Harvey rubbed his forehead. He was deep in thought.

The sound of chopper blades pulsed through the building. Harvey hurried to the front door and stood in the opening, ready to usher in the medics. The rest of us stayed back when the EMTs hustled in with their equipment. They worked quickly, immediately strapping an oxygen mask to Mick's face while they checked his vitals. Then they wasted no time moving him onto a bright orange basket and carrying him out the door. One medic stayed behind briefly, to speak to Harvey and collect the relevant information. Then, just like that, they lifted off and whirred away.

We stood outside, shielding our eyes from the dust. A crowd of onlookers had made their way up from the campsites, to see what was happening. Harvey addressed the group briefly, letting them know what had taken place.

The dirt settled as Mick's ride grew smaller in the bright sky. It was deathly quiet by the time we all turned to one another, unsure of what to do next.

Our leader stepped forward. "Since we're all here, why don't we sit inside and have a meeting?" It felt a little gross, returning to the scene of the incident. But we all mustered the courage and tromped back in together. At least there was no blood to clean up.

"Grab drinks, make yourselves comfortable," Harvey said. He waited until everyone had taken a seat. "First and foremost, I want to thank you all for your quick actions and bravery today. I wasn't here to see everything that took place, but it is clear that you all rose to the occasion. You stayed calm, and in the end, you saved Mick's life. So, thank you." He turned to Stan. "And Stan, what a miracle it was to have a first responder already on the scene and ready to take charge. If you hadn't been here…"

From his seat next to me, Stan objected politely. "If I may, Mr. Watts… Thank you, but Pepper is the one you should be acknowledging." He turned to me with a kind smile. "Pepper took immediate command of the situation. She was cool and calm and told us all what to do, step by step." He took a moment to swallow some emotion. "We just simply listened."

Don't get me wrong, I was gobbling this up. However, it was starting to feel like a Hollywood awards party, where everyone gets together to tell each other how awesome they are. "Thank you, Stan. And Harvey. Everyone here did exactly what they needed to do." I looked around the table, acknowledging each person. "All of you should be proud."

"Yes," Harvey agreed. "Thank you, all. It was certainly a team effort today." Harvey paused and shifted gears. "Now. Before we go on, I need to introduce a special guest." He held his hand out toward my mom, who was sitting beside him. "Everyone, this is Ruth Rose, Pepper's mother. She'll be visiting us for a couple weeks, so please make her feel welcome." Mom smiled and nodded graciously, while everyone muttered short pleasantries.

Harvey took a deep breath. "All right, then. Let's get down to business. Obviously, losing Mick poses quite the challenge. And we've no time to waste in finding a solution." Harvey placed his elbows on the table and clasped his hands together. "This is such a fresh situation...I haven't had any time to think. So, let's open it up for discussion and see if we can't work out the answer together."

Wanda raised her hand. "I can take over for Mick," she said. "If Colt don't mind covering for me at the store..."

Harvey took a moment to consider her proposal. "Yes. Perhaps temporarily. The problem is, Mick will probably be out of commission for a while. So eventually, we'll need Colt for other things.

"And Wanda," I added, "that's a killer job for one person to try and take over. It's too strenuous. Look what it did to Mick."

Mom popped in. "I could help her. I served lunches to over three hundred kids a day for forty years. I think I know my way around a kitchen."

"Oh, Ruth," Harvey interjected. "I'd hate to put you to work."

"I wouldn't mind it a bit. A little action...sounds exciting."

Harvey softened to the idea. "Maybe...I could partner with you, Ruth. We could take turns with Wanda."

"Wait a second, guys. Wait a second," I interrupted. "This is silly. I have the easiest job here. I will take turns in the kitchen with Wanda, and Mom, you can act as camp host." I looked around the table, as people began to nod their heads. Even Harvey raised his eyebrows in consideration.

"May I make a suggestion?" Stan asked politely. "You guys could do a work rotation. Leave Nicole as the waitress and Colt as your fix-it guy. The rest of you work in two-hour blocks, rotating between the kitchen, the store, and the camp host site, which is essentially your rest station. And Mr. Watts, as you already suggested, you would team up with Ruth, since she's a newcomer."

We all sat straighter in our chairs. Harvey looked around, noting our looks of approval. "Stanley, I think you nailed it, sir."

# nine

We took a few minutes to pan out some details. Harvey agreed to print revised menus, to simplify things for us. Mick's nightly dinner specials would be taken off the menu, leaving us with just the short-order items. It was a big compromise for Harvey to make, but I think it was a wise one in the end. I didn't tell him this, but my last meatloaf turned out like dog barf.

Having spelled Mick for a few days after his back injury the previous summer, Wanda was nominated to take the first cooking shift. Thankfully, since we were still in the lunch lull, we had a good hour or two before things picked up. As it turned out, Mick chose the perfect time to drop dead—contrary to what people always say about that sort of thing.

As soon as the meeting broke up, I found my mom and gave her a proper greeting. I embraced her with a long hug and joked, "I hope you didn't think you were coming up here for a vacation!"

She let out a good-hearted laugh. "After spending two months wandering around the house all day and cooking for myself, I think this will be just what I needed." She took a step back and gave me a motherly once-over.

"What?" I whined, preparing to explain the difference between leggings and spandex.

"You look beautiful, Pepper." Her mouth gaped open. "You've lost some weight. And your skin is so smooth and tan." She held out her hands and marveled some more.

I hadn't given it much thought, but I supposed she was right. I was feeling pretty good, and my clothes were starting to fit differently. I'd just figured my pants were getting all stretched out, on account of not doing laundry often enough. As a general rule, I avoided self-reflection of any kind. That included gawking at myself in a mirror. And especially if that mirror happened to be in a dressing room with fluorescent lights directly overhead. For all the money that went into retail marketing, you'd think the clothing industry would figure out how to actually make people look good when they tried on their stuff, instead of accentuating every lump, bump, and hump.

Stan wandered over and stood next to me. He smiled and held out his hand. "Mrs. Rose, I'm Stanley Mann. A friend of Pepper's."

My heart did a little skip, hearing him refer to himself as my friend.

"Hello, Stanley, it's wonderful to meet you."

Harvey joined our group, just as Mom and Stan were finishing their introduction. He placed a hand on Mom's back and said, "Ruth and I were planning to eat when we arrived. Pepper and Stanley, would you care to join us?"

I looked at Stan, who nodded back. "Sure," I answered. "We were just about to fix ourselves some food when… everything happened."

We wandered into the kitchen and scrounged around. I showed Stan where Mick kept Ranger's leftovers bucket. We heaped servings of breakfast slop onto a couple paper plates and set them in the dining room for the dogs. Then Stan and I threw some salads together, while Harvey and Mom opted for turkey and cheese sandwiches, garnished with baggies of potato chips.

The four of us sat at a table near the front, beneath the family photos. "Isn't it just how you remembered, Mom?" I asked.

She nodded while she chewed. "It certainly is," she finally said, with one hand covering her mouth. "Everything has been perfectly preserved. Even that faint maple syrup smell."

Harvey swallowed a bite of his sandwich and said, "Ruth, do you remember the time Pepper crawled into the stinging nettles as a baby?"

"Oh boy, here we go," I said, rolling my eyes.

"That was terrible." Mom shook her head. "The twins had just turned one," she said, wiping her mouth with a napkin. "Jack was supposed to be watching them while I went to the showers. Piper, who started walking at ten months, ran up the road—probably looking for me. While Jack chased after her, Pepper decided to make her great escape. But Pepper was a late walker…" I made a smart-alecky face and mouthed the words, *Pepper was a late walker*, back at my mother. Was there no other way for her to tell this story without humiliating me? She ignored me and continued. "On her way out of Dodge, Pepper managed to crawl right through a stinging nettle bush, wearing nothing but a saggy diaper…" Mom shuddered at the memory. "I could hear her screams all the way from my steaming shower stall. I threw my clothes on as fast as I could and ran to our campsite, leaving a trail of shampoo lather behind. When I got to her, the poor baby was covered in red hot bumps, with the nettles still poking out of her skin, like cactus spines."

Mom had really refined her storytelling, at least with this colorful tale. She had us all wriggling uncomfortably in our seats.

"I didn't know what she'd gotten into. I scooped her up and ran to the store for help. She screamed bloody murder the entire way."

"I was outside the shop," Harvey said, "replacing a rotten board on the deck. I could hear you two coming from a mile away." Harvey smiled at the flashback. I was glad this was such a fond memory for *him*. "I'd seen enough cases of stinging nettles that I knew exactly what we were dealing with. I ran into the store and grabbed a couple packs of tweezers and a box of baking soda…"

"Then he led us behind the buildings and through the back entrance of the kitchen here," Mom said, picking up the rest of the story. "We filled the sink with warm water, dumped in the baking soda, and in you went. Of course, we took your Pampers off before we sat you in there."

*Just what we all needed,* I thought to myself. *A mental image of my bare bottom sliding around the same stainless-steel tub where our dishes are still washed today.*

Harvey tagged back in. "We must have spent an hour picking those nettles out of you."

"They were everywhere," Mom added. "Even between the rolls of your chubby arms and legs. I still have no idea how you managed that…"

Stan could sense my growing embarrassment. He gave me a gentle nudge under the table with his knee. It was a kind gesture. I decided to nudge him back in thanks. Only when I tried it, it turned out to be a wallop. Our knee bones cracked together loudly. We both jumped, wincing in pain.

"What was that?" Mom's head swiveled on high alert, as though hornets might be crawling out of the ground to attack us.

I managed a stiff laugh, even though I was in acute agony. Somehow the pain in my leg was giving me brain-freeze. "It's okay," I said between sharp breaths. "We just banged knees…somehow." I glanced over at Stan, who was grimacing and rubbing his leg—a supposed method of painkilling that never fooled me. Poor guy—I'd really nailed him good. When he finally looked my way, I gave him an apologetic smile.

I could tell by the cute looks on their faces that Mom and Harvey were busily dissecting all the private air waves traveling between me and Stan. And it was mortifying. I felt like a teenager, with the sudden urge to hide my face in my hands and scream, "Make it stop!" The funny thing was, while they were busy reading our body language, I was picking up an awful lot of silent chatter coming from their side of the table as well. I was certain if I dropped my fork on the floor, I might just find the two of them tapping their toes against one another, in some kind of morse code.

We needed a change of subject, *rapido*. "Hey, Mom, did you notice our pictures, still on the Wall of Fame?"

She turned her head. "Oh my." Then she giggled. "Look at those shoulder pads. And my hair! I must have emptied two cans of hairspray to get it to stay up like that… What was I thinking?"

"You were an eighties *momster*," I joked. "Everybody looked like that back then."

Her eyes floated across the old photographs, until they spotted something new. "That picture wasn't there before," she said. She stood in her chair and leaned toward the photo to take a better look. "That's Jack. He must be only seven or eight years old. And that's his mom and dad…" She turned toward Harvey. "Where did this come from?" she asked.

"I found it in one of our family albums a few years back. Decided to put it up with the other Rose pictures." Harvey reached out with his pointer finger. "That's me in there next to Jack. And my mother and father."

"Oh!" Ruth answered with surprise. "I assumed that was one of Jack's cousins. I should have known, though. Look at the two of you, like peas in a pod. You boys must have gotten into a lot of trouble together over the years. I remember Jack talking about that surfing trip you all went on…" Ruth laughed and shook her head. "I can't believe your parents let the two of you go off to Mexico together."

"Wait," I butted in. "Harvey? That was you that went on that trip with Dad?"

"Yes," he said, with a hint of surprise.

"Why didn't he ever mention that?" I asked.

"Who did he say he went with?" Harvey inquired.

"A friend."

"I see," Harvey answered. He carefully placed a potato chip in his mouth and chewed a few times. "So, he talked about the trip…"

"All the time," I answered.

His curiosity grew. "What did he say about it?" Harvey pinched chips out of the bag like an entranced movie-goer, mindlessly munching their popcorn.

I chuckled. "It was the birthplace of his lifelong dream," I answered.

"Which was?" Harvey pressed.

"Loading his family onto a boat and sailing off into the sunset."

Harvey pursed his lips and grunted softly. He gave his bag of chips a gentle shake and peered inside to see what was left. Mom and I glanced at one another, both noting the shift in Harvey's demeanor.

"You remember that story, don't you?" I asked him. "About the Scandinavian family you guys met down there?"

Harvey frowned. "Yes, that's right."

There was a long, uncomfortable pause. Harvey kept his eyes down, while Mom and I made puzzled faces at one another.

"Did something happen on that trip, Harvey?"

Before he could answer, his cell phone rang. Startled, he jumped in his seat before pulling his phone out of his shirt pocket. "It's the hospital," he said. After a swipe of the screen he answered, "Harvey Watts." He listened quietly, as the information on Mick's condition was passed to him. I wasn't sure whether it was the impending news on Mick, or the strange conversation we'd just ended, but something was causing my stomach to churn with anxiety.

When he finished the call, we looked at him expectantly. "He's doing fine," he said, as he placed his phone back in his pocket. "He's regained consciousness, and they don't think surgery will be necessary."

"Thank goodness," Mom replied. We all sat back in our chairs with relief.

"But they do want to keep him for a few days," he said. "And when he does come home, he's got to rest for several weeks. The doctor doesn't want him back in the kitchen for at least another month."

"Sheesh," I replied. "What are we going to do? Should we try to find another cook?"

"No, no," Harvey said. "I'm not going to replace Mick. He needs to know that his job is here waiting for him as soon as he's back on his feet." Harvey took a deep breath. "We'll come up with something."

"You know, I can stay for as long as you need me," Mom replied.

Harvey patted her hand. "Thank you, Ruth." Then he chuckled. "But you haven't even gotten your feet wet. Let's get through one day first, with this new schedule."

Harvey looked at his watch. "Speaking of which, we probably ought to get moving. "Ruth, we need to transport your things down to Pepper's place. Why don't we all hop in the truck, and I'll drive us to the camper."

"Actually, Stan and I will walk the dogs down. You guys go right ahead. We'll meet you there."

We carried our dishes to the kitchen and left them in the sink, to be dealt with later. Watching the plates and cups pile up was a dreadful reminder of all the work that loomed ahead. A small surge of sadness and exhaustion rolled over me as we left the café.

Once we'd gotten down the road a bit, Stan asked, "Are you all right? You got quiet."

"Yeah," I answered. "I'm a little overwhelmed, I think."

"Crazy day."

"Mm-hmm," I agreed. "How's your knee?"

Stan chuckled and answered, "It'll be just fine. How's yours?"

"It's okay. I gave you fair warning, though. I told you I was a klutz."

"You did." He smiled. "I'll make sure to wear my steel-toed shoes, if we ever go dancing together."

"Uh, you might wanna rent one of those sumo suits, as well." Stan broke into a contagious laugh. When it finally died down, we grew quiet once again. A heaviness had returned to my chest. "I guess we'll have to take a rain check on the hot springs, then…"

"Yeah. I should get back to the office."

"So…when do you think you'll be able to make it back out here for another visit?"

"Don't know," he replied. Then he tilted his head toward me and raised one brow. "But with all the drama here lately, I'm thinking Bear Springs might warrant some regular patrols…"

We walked a few more steps. I turned to him sedately and said, "Who says you have to be working?" Stan's face withdrew in surprise. He stared at me perplexed and unable to speak. I smiled back sadly. I was sure I'd scared him.

Off in the distance, I could see Harvey and Mom standing side by side underneath my awning. They looked like an old couple waiting on the train platform: Mom with her suitcase on the ground next to her and a large bouquet of flowers in her hands. Both were looking our way. Before we got any closer, Stan took a gentle hold of my arm and came to a halt. We turned and faced one another. I could feel his warm hand cupping my elbow. "I would really like that, Pepper," he said softly.

As much as I wanted to be engulfed in the moment, I was feeling extremely distracted by the four ogling eyeballs up ahead. Flustered, I stuck out my hand and replied, "Okay then." Stan looked quizzically at my outstretched arm. He slowly repeated, "Okay then," and reached out hesitantly to shake on it. After an uneasy moment, we both turned and continued walking.

Of course, I was immediately sickened with myself. But it could have been worse. Instead of the handshake, I could've instinctively heeled him in the fanny as we walked along. Surely *that* would have shaken Harvey and Mom right off our tracks. Ugh.

When we reached my camper, Stan said a quick good-bye to everyone and loaded Cinnamon into her seat. As he walked around the front of the truck, he gave us a final wave. I caught his eye and mouthed, "Call me." He tipped his hat with a caring smile and climbed behind the wheel.

Harvey picked up Mom's suitcase and dropped it inside. He came back down the steps and said, "I'm going to head up the road. How about if I meet you ladies in my office in an hour, ready to work?"

"See you in an hour," I said. Mom and I waved goodbye to Harvey before climbing into the trailer.

"Isn't this lovely?" she said, taking her first peek inside. "Spacious, neat and tidy..."

"Not a lot of room for clutter, so that helps," I said. She wandered through the trailer on her own, still clutching the flowers in her hand.

"Someone stopped at the flower shop before they picked you up," I teased. I reached into the small cabinet space under the sink and pulled out the clear glass vase I'd received from Harvey when I arrived.

"You were certainly right about him," she said, with a twinkle in her eye. She drifted back in my direction. I slid a pair of scissors across the counter to her. She unwrapped the bouquet and began expertly snipping the ends of the stalks at precise angles.

"What do you mean?" I filled the vase with water and set it down in front of her.

"He is an absolute gem." Mom placed the flowers into their new home and fussed with them a bit, making sure they all looked even, or…something.

I laughed and plopped heavily onto the small sofa, whose cushions were still stiff from unuse. "Whew. I am exhausted," I said. "How about you? You doing okay?"

"I think so. My head is spinning though. I feel like so much has happened, and I haven't had time to process any of it." She left the bouquet on the counter and sat down next to me. "I went from zero stimulation to over-stimulation."

"You sure did."

"It sounds like Mick is going to be all right, though. That's a huge relief."

"It's a miracle," I said. "He was clinically dead, Mom. I didn't think we were going to be able to revive him."

"Oh my goodness. Does Harvey know that?"

"I don't think so. Everything has happened so fast. I feel like this is the first moment we've had to catch our breath."

"I'm sure he'll want to know all the details, once things settle down."

"Yeah," I said, feeling my attention shift. I sighed. "What did you think about that whole surfing trip thing, with Harvey and Daddy? How weird was that?"

"Mm, I don't know. I wasn't sure what to make of that."

"Do *you* know something?" I turned in my seat to look at her directly.

"What? No!" She threw both hands into the air, pleading innocence.

"You obviously knew more than I did. I never knew it was Harvey that he'd gone with. Why would Daddy hide that from me?"

"Oh, I don't think he was hiding anything from you, honey."

"Harvey seemed to think it was weird. And he was keen to know what Daddy had shared with me about their trip."

"I'm sure it was nothing. They probably had too much to drink one night, and had a spat over a girl, or something silly like that."

"I don't know. That doesn't sound like Daddy. Or Harvey."

"Well, it's all water under the bridge now. They obviously moved past whatever it was and got along fine afterwards."

I raised my eyebrows. "I guess so."

# ten

Mick was released from the hospital one week later. Harvey had visited him a few days earlier, to bring him a care package of goodies, and a card we'd all signed. Now the boss had left again, to bring Mick home.

Mom proved to be a quick study and was doing fine during Harvey's brief absences. The biggest challenge for her so far was the long hours. Even I was having a hard time adjusting to being on the go from 8 a.m. to 8 p.m. I sure did come to appreciate the camp host position, though. We all did. In fact, with Wanda now getting a taste of the good life, I was a little worried she might become resentful of my situation, once things returned to normal.

Even though it was strenuous, I did find myself appreciating the work rotation. I was glad to learn the ins and outs of running the store, as well as the cafe. And even more so, I was enjoying the solidarity I was building with the other staff.

Wanda and I were getting to know each other better through our brief interactions every two hours when we had to switch stations. We started swapping books, and we had a little spy ring going on. She and I were gathering intelligence on the budding romance between Harvey and Mom. The two were connected at the hip and were constantly pinching each other's shoulders and whatnot. It was a little weird to see Mom acting like that with another man, but she deserved to have a friend. And so did Harvey.

I was behind the register at the store when I heard Harvey's truck pull in behind the shop. I didn't have any customers, so I popped outside with Ranger to welcome Mick home before he walked to his cabin.

I slowed my steps as I cornered the rear of the truck. Mick was holding onto the grab bar, contemplating how to get both feet smoothly to the ground. I was shocked to see how fragile he looked, especially with the hospital bracelet still dangling from his wrist. He'd lost a lot of muscle tone lying in that bed all week.

Ranger was thrilled to see Mick. He ran to the open door and stood on his hind legs to greet him. Mick remained in his seat, helpless against Ranger's affections.

"Ranger, get down," I said. Harvey clapped his hands together, coaxing Ranger to leave Mick alone. Harvey stepped in and helped Mick ease out of the truck.

"Hey, big guy, nice to see you on your feet," I finally said.

He turned slowly. "Oh, hey," he said quietly. He gathered a weak smile.

I opened my arms and gently hugged him. Hospital odors clung to his skin, and his unshaven bristles scratched my cheek.

"Harvey told me what you did for me," he said as we separated. "Thank you." He lowered his head.

"I was glad we were there to help." Harvey stepped closer and put a supporting hand on Mick's back. "I won't hold you fellas up. Just wanted to welcome you home. It's wonderful to have you back."

"Thanks, Pepper," Mick said. He shuffled up the dirt path with Harvey at his side. I watched a few more seconds, still startled by his condition. I was also struck by the fact that he had no luggage with him. He returned just as simply as he had gone; the only differences being a new t-shirt, and the small white pharmacy bag that Harvey was carrying for him. I silently wished Mick a speedy recovery. But something told me he had a long road ahead of him.

It was two days later, the middle of the afternoon, and Nicole and I were the only people in the café. I decided to take some food to Mick and see how he was getting on. Harvey had been looking in on him regularly, but I figured Mick might appreciate seeing another friendly face now and then. I left the restaurant in Nicole's care and went to pay the convalescent a quick visit.

I knocked on his door and called out, "Hey, Mick, it's Pepper. And Ranger."

"Come in," he said. I tried to open the door slowly, to give him time to situate himself for company. But as soon as I made a crack, Ranger wedged his big lab head in there and blasted the thing open like a battering ram. The doorknob bounced off the interior wall with a loud *pop*.

"Sorry about that…" I stepped inside, where Mick was outstretched in an old Lay-Z-Boy chair. Ranger was already at his side, panting hot dog breath all over him. "Oh, Ranger! Leave him alone."

Mick had smartly drawn his knees up in a defensive posture, just in case my dog, who was no longer a little puppy, decided to spring into his lap. "It's okay. He's fine." Mick grabbed the television remote and lowered the volume on the baseball game he was watching.

"Didn't know if you might be hungry," I said, holding up a to-go container. "I made you a hot Reuben with extra cheese, extra sauce, and some onion rings on the side."

He chuckled. "Not sure my doc would approve..."

"Eh," I said with a shrug. "That's what the pills are for. Enjoy."

He opened the Styrofoam box and took a sniff. He popped an onion ring in his mouth and said, "Pull up a seat."

"All right. I can't stay long, though." I borrowed his desk chair and scooted it around. "You're looking better," I said.

"Thanks."

I glanced around the room, hoping to find a conversation piece. But his cabin was stark. There were no photos or other personal items lying in sight. I'd been curious to learn more about Mick, especially after Harvey mentioned his background as one of Tim's defendants. But the guy was like a bank vault.

"I...noticed your Semper Fi tattoo," I ventured courageously. "How long were you in the Marines?"

"Four years." He focused his eyes on the television and ate a few more onion rings. I kept quiet, hoping he'd offer more info.

"Was it not a good fit?"

"Nope. I got out, moved back to Fresno. Got wind about the job up here from Tim Watts."

"Oh, how'd you know Tim?" I was on a slippery slope here and started to feel a bit guilty.

"He and I went to high school together."

"Oh really? I hadn't heard that." No, I had heard a different version, for sure. "You and Tim were friends, then?"

"Teammates. Played on the football team together." I nodded, silently begging for more. But I don't think he saw me. I had lost his attention to the baseball game, where grown men in furry animal costumes were racing one another around the bases. That sport sure had to go to great lengths to keep their fans entertained.

He snapped out of his trance once the race was over. "I was two years older than him. Tim was a standout. He was one of the team captains as a sophomore, when I was a senior."

That sounded about right. "I bet that made some of your teammates jealous, huh?"

"It ruffled a few feathers. But deep down, the guys admired him. Tim was one of those kids—an overachiever. We all knew he was headed for success."

I was impressed with myself for having gotten Mick to talk. Since he was virtually spewing with information, I decided to push for more. "How'd you end up reconnecting with him, after all those years?"

His mouth twitched. He dropped his eyes to his lap, where his hands were fidgeting with the remote. "Tim helped me out of a bind. I'd…been through a rough patch."

"I see."

He cleared his throat. "I try not to dwell on the past, though." Mick swallowed hard. Then he turned his head and looked at me with a broken smile. Through his tired naked eyes, I saw honesty and vulnerability. And anguish.

Before me sat a deeply wounded man on the brink of baring his soul. For a nosey old busy body like myself, this was nothing short of pay dirt. One little shove, and I could've had Mick spilling his guts. But somehow, it didn't feel right. For one thing, I wasn't sure his heart could take it. And also, I was feeling the odd urge to be respectful.

"Hey, I'd better let you get some rest." I stopped by his chair on my way out and gave his hand a pump. "Let me know if you need anything."

"Sure. Thanks for stopping by. And thanks again for… giving me a second chance."

I smiled softly. "Everyone deserves a second chance."

Ranger and I returned to the café through the back entrance. As soon as I stepped into the kitchen, I could hear Harvey's voice coming from the dining area. I glanced at the wall clock. We still had forty-five minutes before Harvey and Mom were supposed to relieve me. Before I could figure out what was going on, Ranger darted to the front room, all excited. I followed.

When the room came into view, I saw Nicole seated at a table, patting her eyes with a napkin. Then I saw Harvey, conversing quietly with Stan. Cinnamon approached me sweetly, with her ears back and tail swaying side to side. "Hi, baby," I whispered. I kneeled to greet her, while I listened in to get a read on what was happening.

The boys finally noticed me and stopped their conversation abruptly. "Pepper," Harvey said, sounding very somber. "Stan has come with some news." Adrenaline coursed through my body, preparing me for a jolt.

Stan took a step toward me, holding his hat in front of him. "They found a body in Juniper Lake." He paused and softened his voice. "We think it may be Trevor." I stood there in both shock and relief, thankful we weren't beginning a brand-new crisis. I replayed the message in my head.

"Juniper Lake? Where's that?"

"Forty miles east, down the mountain."

I scrunched up my face. "I thought he disappeared at *Harris* Lake, though. That doesn't make any sense."

"We're baffled as well."

"And you're sure it's him?"

"Pretty sure. The body's been badly…" Stan glanced at Nicole and cut himself off. "The general description matches Trevor," he said, scratching a nervous itch on the back of his neck. "I dropped by to ask Mr. Watts to view the remains. See if we could get a positive I.D."

Harvey stood with his shoulders slumped and hands shoved into his pockets. I felt horrible for him. How much more could he take? "Are you up for it, Harv?" I asked with pity. But it wasn't like he had a choice.

"Yes, yes," he said, nodding at the floor. He gave himself a moment, before raising his chin and clasping his hands together in self-determination. "Let's get it done, then. Why don't I follow you in my car, Stanley, so you don't have to come all the way back out here?"

"No, sir, I'll drive you." Stan shifted his feet. "I really don't mind." Stan flashed me a quick look.

I held back a grin. "See you guys later then," I said, as they meandered toward the exit. I stood and peered out from behind the screen door. As they crossed the dirt lot toward the Forest Service truck, Stan reached over and gave Harvey's shoulder a squeeze.

❋ ❋ ❋

It was quarter after seven when the guys pulled in outside the store. I was in the shop sweeping the floor, getting ready to close things up for the night. Anxious for the update, I carried my broom out the door and waved at them from the porch. Ranger, who was now familiar with the sight and sound of Stan and Cinnamon's work vehicle, ran across the road to greet them.

With the low-lying sun lighting them from behind, the men's expressions were difficult to read as they made their approach. Their footsteps were heavy on the hollow stairs.

"Well?" I looked from face to face, waiting for a response. The guys moved closer, creating a tight triangle. They both looked ragged.

Harvey took a deep breath and said, "It was him."

Stan waited respectfully before adding, "Mr. Watts was able to confirm a tattoo on the left forearm. Even though it was pretty messed up."

I nodded silently.

"And I recognized the boot that was still on his…remaining foot," Harvey added, with a pained look on his face.

I closed my eyes out of sheer sorrow. Not only for Trevor, but also for these two brave men. Like the stench of death, the images were just as foul, and tended to linger.

"There was a lot of damage, due to being in the water so long," Stan clarified.

"Is there any evidence to indicate cause of death?" I asked.

"Not that we could see. That'll be up to the medical examiner."

"Assuming this was a drug deal gone bad," I mused, "I'm wondering if they killed him before moving his body to the other lake? Or if he willingly got into their vehicle?"

"Good questions," Stan said.

"Transporting a body like that—it's not only risky, but it leaves behind a lot of evidence."

"Hopefully the autopsy can shed some light. But when we scoped out Harris Lake, we found no blood, no signs of struggle, nothing to suggest he'd been killed there, or kidnapped even."

"What about Juniper Lake? Did they search that area for evidence?"

"The county guys looked around, but honestly, if there was a crime scene there… It's been two months. With all the people tromping around, the animals, the elements… It's unlikely much would be preserved."

"Hmm." I pondered. "What about Trevor's car? What was that like when you found it? Was the door open? Closed? Did it look like anyone had rifled through his things?"

"The car was all buttoned up. Door was not only closed, but locked. As far as his belongings… He wasn't what I would call a *neat packer*, so it's tough to say for sure. But it didn't look like his personal affects had been gone through."

I thought out loud. "Which suggests to me that the deal didn't take place in the parking area. It sounds like he parked the car, got out, locked the doors, and then walked to a meeting place, presumably in the woods somewhere."

"Or down by the water," Stan suggested.

"What about his car keys? Did they show up?"

"Haven't been found," Stan said. "And they weren't on the body."

Harvey had remained quiet during our discussion. I looked over and found him staring at the deck, completely withdrawn. I shot Stan a look and said, "I bet you boys haven't had any supper yet. Why don't you go next door for some food before it all gets put away? Get something for Cinnamon as well."

Stan nodded. "Good idea. I'll come find you when we're done." Then, with a gentle touch, he prompted Harvey to turn and head toward the café.

❀

# <u>eleven</u>

I had just cashed the tills and was entering the numbers into the daily balance sheet, when Stan returned from dinner. "Hey there," I said. "I'll be done in a sec…" He and Cinnamon wandered around the store with Ranger on their heels, while I finished my paperwork. After I made my last note, I carried the worksheet along with the cash drawer back to Harvey's office, where we locked everything up each night.

When I reemerged, I found Stan in the camping section, scrutinizing a package he'd pulled from the shelf. "How is this a towel?" he asked, as I came up behind him.

"It's a travel towel," I answered. "For hiking and camping."

"It looks like a sponge."

"I think it gets bigger after you wet it."

"Like a grow monster?"

"A what?"

"You know, expandable water toys. Didn't you have those as a kid? The pre-historic creatures that you keep in a bowl for several days…"

I shook my head. "Uh, no."

"I'm afraid you missed out."

I laughed. "I sincerely doubt it."

"They have an interesting history. They're made from a superabsorbent polymer, which was invented in the 1960s by scientists at the USDA—the department the Forest Service falls under, by the way…"

"Why was the Department of Agriculture making this stuff?"

"They were looking for a substance that could help soil conserve water."

"Huh. And why do you know this?"

"My dad was a science and nature buff. That man could tell you anything you wanted to know about plants, animals, rock formations… He taught me almost everything I know. Anyway, would it mess you up if I bought this right now?" He held up the towelette.

I chuckled. "Why? Are you going to grow it in your bathtub? Or are you actually in need of a towel? Cuz if you are, I'd be happy to lend you a real one…"

"I might need one," he said, with a guilty grin. I squinted my eyes at him suspiciously. "I threw my swim shorts in the truck a couple days ago, just in case we ever got the chance to take that dip in the hot springs…"

"Stanley Mann, you sly little devil."

"Are you doing anything right now?"

I shook my head with surprise. "I am free as a bird. What about you? Are you off-duty? Or is there such a thing?"

He chuckled. "I am off the clock. And it's a Friday night." He wiggled his eyebrows at me.

"Well, put that silly thing back on the shelf and let's get outta here!"

❀ ❀ ❀

Dusk was quickly turning to night as we piled into the truck with the two dogs and drove down to my camper. Mom was inside, getting herself ready for bed.

"I just got off the phone with Harvey," she said, as we came through the door. "He gave me the sad news about Trevor."

"How did he sound to you?" I asked. "Because he seemed fairly distraught when he got back."

"He's all right. It's just the stress of Mick getting sick, and all the extra responsibilities. And now with Trevor…" She smiled sadly. "He wants to have a little memorial service for him."

"How? We can't all leave Bear Springs in the middle of the season to go to a service."

"He wants to do something small. Maybe at the river."

"Oh. That's sweet of Harvey."

"It's just Harvey," Mom replied bluntly. She filled a glass of water at the kitchen sink and took a sip. "What are you two up to?"

"We're on our way to the hot springs."

"At this hour? It's nearly dark!"

"Mom, we used to do that all the time. Don't you remember?"

"Not me. I wasn't doing any river crossings in the dark. Or tromping through the weeds. I like to see what snakes I'm stepping on."

"But that's part of the fun. Anyway, we're bringing flash-lights. And we'll have the dogs with us. They can run ahead and scare all the critters away."

She shivered with disgust. "You kids have a good time. I'm so tired, I may be asleep before you even get your swimsuits on."

"All right, goodnight," I said, with a light chuckle. "Stan, you wanna get changed in the bathroom?"

"Sure," he replied.

"See you in a minute," I said, retreating to my bedroom. As soon as I shut the door behind me, I felt like I was trapped in one of those recurring dreams, where the school bus is pulling up outside your house, and you're still searching your drawers for one missing sock. Even though I knew Stan wouldn't leave without me, I began frantically rushing around my room, trying to undress and locate my bathing suit at the same time.

My heart was still beating wildly when I flung the door open. Stan was a few paces away. He was turned to the side, quietly reviewing the jacket of one of my novels. The image only lasted a moment, but seeing him out of his uniform for the first time made an imprint. He stood there looking so relaxed and ordinary, with his furry white tummy hanging over his waistband and his dinosaur toes floating off the edge of his cheap plastic flip-flops. I was enamored.

I strode out of my room in my toad-green one-piece, looking just as unromantic and equally unashamed.

Stan looked up from the book. "All set?"

"Yep, I'll just grab a couple towels and flashlights."

The quickest way to the river was a pathway that cut through the middle of the campground, past the restrooms. We set off in our towels and flip-flops, looking like hotel guests in search of the pool. We kept our flashlights off, enjoying the remaining bits of light outside. Overhead, the sky was losing its last hints of blue. While our eyes adjusted to the darkness, our other senses came alive. A cool evening breeze carried the sweet smell of the pines, while the scent of the campfires seemed to hang unaffected in the air.

This had become my favorite time of day at Bear Springs—when the families reconvened around the warm glow of their fires to engage in snack time, or story time, or game time. It was an ageless ritual, when the earth dimmed its celestial lights, forcing mankind to our shelters to create our own illuminations, and to focus on the faces beside us.

Stan and I flipped on our flashlights as we neared the river's edge. "The water won't come above our calves here, but the rocks are very slippery," I warned. "You'll want to take your sandals off." Ranger and Cinnamon entered the shallow water, lapping as they went. I picked up my flip-flops and proceeded cautiously ahead of Stan.

"Walking sticks would've been a good idea," he said.

I could hear the water whooshing around his legs as he took his first few steps into the tiny rapids. With my feet firmly planted, I looked back to see him waving his arms in a clumsy balancing act. "Hey, you're blinding me!"

"Oops! Sorry," I giggled. I lowered my beam of light and waited until he got closer. "Here, take my hand." Both Stan and I were well outside our comfort zones, putting our physical dexterities to the test. I'm not sure what made me think holding on to each other would help the situation any, but, like a hypothermic person that ditches all their clothing, we did what seemed right in the moment. Stan reached out and grasped my free hand with his. I felt a rush of energy flow through me, leaving me with a delightful sensation that lasted about one-point-three seconds, after which, I lost my balance and bucked backwards with a Samson-like violence that brought the whole house down. Shoes and flashlights flew like confetti, blasted from a party store gun.

I splashed straight onto my tooshie, while Stan took a hard, horizontal plunge.

I dared not move, petrified by my life-long fear of a shattered coccyx—an unfortunate anxiety resulting from one overheard conversation at my mother's hair salon when I was a tender child.

Stan spewed water from his mouth and pushed himself into a crawling position. "Pepper, are you all right?"

"I think so." I gently lifted my hips, waiting to be stricken by searing pain. "How about you?"

He let out a playful laugh. "I'm fine. But our shoes are long gone, and our towels are soaked." He pointed and laughed again. "And the flashlights are literally dead in the water!"

"Oh no! I'm so sorry. Do you want to go back?"

"No way." Stan's voice became animated. "This is our Rubicon, Pepper." He raised a fist out of the water. "Let the die be cast!"

I chuckled with glee, watching him emerge from his shell. "Okay, whoever you are. But first I have to get out of this towel before it anchors me to the riverbed." I grunted and pulled, until I freed my waist from the water-logged towel. I passed it to Stan, who steadied himself on his knees and lobbed both towels onto the shore behind us. "And now, we just need to figure out how to get back on our feet."

"I'm going to stay just the way I am." Stan crawled around me in a circle, showing off his newfound mobility.

"That's not a bad idea." I remained in my sitting position and began to crab-walk alongside him. "Slow down, hot shot!"

We must have looked ridiculous, inching our way across the current on all fours. After several tedious minutes, we dragged our out-of-shape bodies into the grassy weeds along the embankment and sat to catch our breath.

As we rested, I glanced around and noticed that we were sitting in a field of white flowers. "Look!" I said, turning in my seat. "Where did all these flowers come from? Why have I never noticed these here before?"

Stan plucked one from its stem and held it in front of me. "Because during the day, they're just green weeds. But as soon as the sun starts to go down, their petals open up."

"Night-blooming flowers?"

"Mm-hmm. These are called moon flowers."

"They're amazing." I took the flower head from Stan and studied it as best I could in the limited light. "What a beautiful creation."

Stan picked another bloom and gently placed it above my ear. "Very beautiful."

His compliment caught me off guard. And while I was pretty sure he was directing his admiration toward me and not the flower, I wasn't willing to risk the humiliation. His comment dangled in the air for several restless moments, while I debated my response. I needed to convey something unpresumptuous but appreciative. Would a Mona Lisa smile do that? No, too stony. I shook my head and went back to the drawing board.

"Whatcha doin' over there?"

"Huh?" I turned my head sharply toward Stan. "Oh geez. I wasn't talking out loud, was I?"

Stan's face broke into a beaming smile. "Do you know the most beautiful thing about these flowers, Miss Rose?"

I cast my eyes toward my lap. "What?"

"Watching them open up."

My face turned to his. Even though his lips had closed, his eyes were smiling on, sparkling and serene, like a moon-lit river.

When I finally found my voice, it was low and smokey. "Sounds like we'll have to come back out here again. To see that."

Stan cocked his head. "Is that a date, then?" he asked coolly.

"If that's what they still call it."

Stan slowly rose to his feet. He stood in front of me and held out his hands. When I took them, he gently raised me up until we were face to face. With my hands in his, he said, "Well, my lady, Julius Caesar's crossing may have been a tad more graceful than ours. But I dare say, ours was every bit as memorable."

I smiled wistfully and then grew quiet. "Our Rubicon moment, was it?"

He dipped his head toward mine and whispered, "Point of no return."

※ ※ ※

Though we were cold, wet, and in the dark, Stan and I set forth with youthful spirits to find the nearest hot spring. We forged our way down the trampled path, feeling the spongy bog beneath our bare feet, until we saw steam rising from the earth.

At Bear Springs, some of the hot pools were left in their natural mud bath state, while others had been walled with concrete, creating a far less messy experience. Thankfully, we had arrived at one of these. Stan and I sat on the edge and eased in carefully, enjoying the immediate gratification of the heat.

"Wow," Stan marveled. "This is amazing. Look at the stars!" I lifted my head and felt the instant sensation of being seated in the center of a 3-D IMAX theatre. I could see the entire circle of the sky, like a domed ceiling arcing over me. The stars appeared so bright and close, I wanted to catch them in my hand and put them in a jar.

"It is a work of art," I replied with awe.

"Perfectly and wonderfully made."

"Mm," I replied, with an acquiescent nod. We meditated quietly for a few moments.

"What do you think happened to Trevor?" I asked.

He furrowed his brow. "What made you go there all the sudden?"

"I don't know. Just pondering the mysteries of life, I guess."

"Oh." He skimmed his hand across the top of the water. "I do actually have a theory, but…"

"What is it?"

"Promise you won't laugh?"

"I don't make promises. But I will try not to laugh. And I will try not to pee in this water when I try not to laugh. But just so you know…that sort of stunt can be tough for gals my age." He crossed his arms and tilted his head. "Stan, I'm just kidding. Please, your theory is safe with me. Go right on ahead."

He looked like a young boy on the edge of the high dive. With eyes widening ever so slightly, he took a deep breath and muttered, "I believe Trevor was killed, dumped into Harris Lake, and then sucked into a subterranean river, which transported him down the mountain through over forty miles of underground water caverns, before spewing him out into Juniper Lake."

I stared at him blankly for several seconds. Then I slapped my hand across my mouth and started dancing on my toes, causing small waves to lap out of the tank. "Ohhh…."

Stan stood upright with alarm. "What is it?"

"I'm trying not to peeee…"

Stan chuckled humorlessly. "Pepper," he whined. "See? I told you. I knew you would laugh."

"No, no. I'm sorry. I'm not making fun of your theory. It's just…" A giggle snuck out. "You're so cute when you get all serious and nerdy like that."

"Serious and nerdy? Great."

"I told you, though. I think it's charming. It's very… Indiana Jones."

Stan seemed impressed with that. "Well then," he said in acceptance.

"Tell me more about this theory. How did you come up with it?"

"Honestly, it was the first thing that popped into my head, the moment I heard he'd been found in another lake. My dad used to tell me stories about an unexplained phenomenon that occurs not too far from here."

I leaned forward. "What is it?"

"People that have disappeared into the waters of Lake Tahoe sometimes show up sixty-one miles away, at Pyramid Lake."

"That's weird."

"It gets weirder. Because the same thing happens in reverse. The bodies of people that've disappeared from Pyramid Lake, have been discovered in Lake Tahoe."

"What in the world?"

"I know it sounds totally far-fetched, but the underground river theory is actually the most reasonable explanation for these occurrences. But unfortunately, these stories always get lumped in with all the other mystical legends about those lakes."

My face crinkled. "What other legends?"

"Like the belief that the bottom of Lake Tahoe is a secret graveyard, filled with bodies that have been perfectly preserved over time."

"Eew. That's not true, is it?"

"It's entirely possible. Tahoe's over 1600 feet deep. At its lower depths, the water temperature maintains a steady thirty-nine degrees, which is cold enough to halt the body's normal putrefaction process. And this makes the lake a perfect dumping ground for bodies, because the people who put them there never have to worry about the corpses filling with gas and floating to the surface."

"Are you making this crap up?"

"No! I'm dead serious. You've never heard the stories about the mob filling casino buckets with concrete and tying them to their victims before dumping them in the middle of the lake?"

I shook my head.

"There's that other one, too—about Jacques Cousteau. Rumor has it, he once did a deep dive at Tahoe. And when he came up, he was so disturbed by what he saw that he refused to talk about it. All he said was, 'The world is not ready for what I have seen.'"

"That's creepy." I was feeling a strong urge to draw my feet up from the muddy floor, closer to the rest of me.

"You should hear the stories about Pyramid Lake. Those are even worse."

My eyes doubled in size. "They are?"

"People have reported all kinds of weird sightings there, like mermaids, and the ghosts of the soldiers who fought the Paiute Indians in the Pyramid Lake War. That lake is even said to be haunted by *water babies*."

"Water babies?"

"The deformed or prematurely born Paiute infants, who were thrown into the lake to die. People say the spirits of those babies can still be heard laughing and crying."

"Stan, you're trying to scare me!" I reached out and slapped his arm.

He laughed and put his hands up in innocence. "I am not making this up!"

"How did we get to telling ghost stories, then?"

"I was getting back around to Trevor," he said, looking pleased with his ability to command the audience. "It's simple. The mountains and lakes in this region share the same history and geology. If Tahoe and Pyramid are connected by underground rivers, then Harris and Juniper could be as well."

"But if there's no way to prove the underground passageways exist, then there's no way to confirm your hypothesis about Trevor."

"You're right, unfortunately. Even if we eliminated every other possible explanation of how he got from one place to the other…it still doesn't prove my theory to be true. And more importantly, it doesn't tell us who killed him."

# twelve

A week had passed since Stan and I made our dramatic river crossing and acknowledged the relationship we were growing. It was now Saturday afternoon, and I was sitting alone under my awning, letting the rainstorm draw me into a more wholly despondent state. Stan had called a couple days earlier to say that a last-minute slot had opened for a K-9 search and rescue course. He and Cinnamon were leaving on Sunday, right after Trevor's memorial, and would be gone for two weeks. I don't know why it was bothering me so much—it wasn't like we saw each other that often. I think it was just the timing of it. He was like a marvelous gift I'd just unwrapped, only to discover that it needed to be sent back to the factory.

A loud crack of thunder brought me back to the present. The storms here were extraordinary. With Bear Springs situated in the center of a topographical bowl, our thunder and lightning would get caught between the mountains and roll back and forth, giving us an amazing display of weather. I eased out of my seat and walked to the edge of the awning to peek at the sky. Earlier today, the storm clouds had been dark and heavy with moisture. But now, it looked like we were inside the clouds themselves.

A golf cart appeared, heading my way. It was most likely Colt, going to unclog a drain. The cart splashed through a giant puddle and pulled up next to me.

"Mick?" I almost didn't recognize him, out of context like this.

"Hey, Pepper. Harvey told me you'd be down here." He reached out to pet Ranger's head.

My brain was so confused. "Is everything okay?"

"Yeah." Mick stepped out of the cart, which was being pelted by rain. He ducked his head and stepped under the awning with me. We faced one another awkwardly.

"Would you like to come inside?"

"I was gonna see if you wanted to take a walk, actually."

This was getting weirder by the second. My eyes betrayed me, bulging with bewilderment.

"I brought umbrellas," he offered. "They're nice and big."

"Um…okay. Sure." My anxiety was spiking. If he dragged me into the woods and offed me, I was gonna be really PO'd at myself.

Mick took two oversized golf umbrellas out of the cart and handed one to me. Thunder rumbled across the sky. "I love walking in the rain," he said.

"Me, too," I lied. Actually, I didn't mind the getting wet part so much. It was the becoming a human lightning rod bit that I found distasteful. I popped open my umbrella. "All set? Did you need anything before we set off?" *Duct tape? Hefty bag?*

"Nope."

"C'mon, Ranger," I said, as a subtle reminder that I had a secret weapon on my side. *Ha ha.* We stepped into the rainfall, which created a noisy drumming on our umbrellas. "I guess you're clear to do some light exercise now, huh?"

"Yup. Supposed to walk every day."

We slopped past several campsites, which were looking dismal in the downpour. A few people had the foresight to hang tarps over their tents and picnic areas. But for the others, it was going to be a miserable night trying to keep the bedding dry. "Café's going to be busy this evening."

"Oh yeah," he agreed. "It's probably already full of people, just looking for a dry place to sit."

"You got that right," I answered, feeling grateful for my cozy RV.

"I was hoping to talk to you about something," he finally said.

So there *was* a purpose behind this. That was a relief—I was starting to think I'd been selected to be his new exercise partner.

"When you came to visit me, we got to talking about second chances," he said. "And these past few weeks have forced me to do a lot of thinking. Thinking about…turning a new page in life." I remained quiet and let him speak. "So first of all, I wanted to correct something I told you that day."

"Oh," I said with surprise. "All right…"

"When I said I'd done four years with the Marines, that wasn't exactly true. I went AWOL three years in. Ended up with an Other than Honorable Discharge."

"I see."

"I'm sorry for being less than honest with you."

"That's all right," I answered, worried that it was now my turn to fess up to my fib about enjoying walking in the rain.

"Thing is, there's a lotta stuff connected to that. Things I've been running from. But…I don't think I can run anymore."

I turned to read his expression, but the enormous umbrella was hiding his face like a travelling confessional.

I began to imagine wartime scenes, where soldiers were forced to do unmentionables, in order to stay alive. I was more than curious about the coming revelation, but I decided to heed Harvey's advice. I kept quiet and gave Mick the space he needed. We continued, my shoes now making embarrassing squishing noises with each step.

"I was stationed at Pendleton," he began. "Everything was going pretty good. I was young and fit. I had friends, a cool job…even had a steady girl. One weekend, a bunch of us decided to go down to Tijuana to party. We weren't supposed to, but everybody did it. My girlfriend came along. Anyway, after we'd been there a while, we decided to leave the bar and look for another club. There were five of us. As we were walking down the street, we got jumped. I don't know how many of them there were, but it was an ambush. My buddies and I fought as hard as we could. One of my friends pulled out a knife. Things got bloody. We hurt some of those Mexicans pretty bad. But we were completely outnumbered. In the end, they got what they came for. They took my girlfriend."

"She was kidnapped?" My mouth hung open in disbelief.

Mick slowed to a stop, visibly impacted by the weight of his admission. Under the rim of the umbrella, I could make out the bottom of his wrinkled chin, trembling with emotion.

I softened my tone and asked, "What did you guys do?"

He began to cry lightly. "What do you think? Under-aged soldiers sneaking across the border to get drunk? Then wounding, possibly killing, guys in a knife fight? We ran, Pepper."

"But what about your girlfriend?" The rain increased its intensity as Mick shook his head and began to sob freely. "Did you go to the authorities?"

"That's what I'm telling you. We left her. We left her behind!"

I watched him weep openly, and I felt numb inside. His sobs eventually softened, until they resembled a low moan. Mick clutched at his chest with his left hand. He slowly clawed at the shirt collar and pulled downward, until the tattoo over his heart could be seen. "Semper Fi. Do you know what that means, Pepper? Always faithful. Always loyal." He let out a wounded, sardonic laugh.

"So, you and the three other guys returned to your car and drove back to the base?"

"Yeah."

"And?"

"And we made a pact."

My gut wrenched. "What about the girl's parents? Did anyone ever try to contact them?"

He looked at the muddy road and shook his head in shame. He began to move forward again.

"That's an awfully big load to carry."

"It wasn't easy for any of us. My buddy, the one with the knife, ended up committing suicide the next year. Not long after that, I walked away. Moved back to Fresno, turned to alcohol. Ended up in jail with a DUI. That's how Tim and I got back in touch."

"Mick. I'm so sorry that happened to you. Did you ever find out what became of her? What is her name?"

"Lina. No. I was too scared. Didn't want to know. When I got outta jail, I landed this job. It was the perfect place to lay low and…hide from my past."

I could feel the scales slowly tipping in my direction, as Mick unburdened himself for what I presumed was the first time. That made me one of four remaining people who knew what had happened to this girl—even though her fate remained a mystery. "Telling someone is a really big step," I said, with a heavy heart. "Are you…thinking about doing more?"

"I'd like to. I need to put this behind me somehow. But I wouldn't know where to start. I've never even owned a computer."

"Would you like some help?"

He tilted his umbrella back and looked at me with desperate, bloodshot eyes. "I'd be grateful."

❋ ❋ ❋

After I finished work that evening, I sat at my table, looking over the notes I'd taken after Mick and I finished our walk. He hadn't given me much to go on.

"Lina Ortiz, 18, resident of Oceanside, California. Abducted in Tijuana, Mexico in the early hours of Saturday, March 4, 1988."

I opened my laptop and pulled up the site for the National Missing and Unidentified Persons System. I typed in her name and hit "enter." The answer to my query popped up instantly: "Zero records matching your search."

I wanted to pick up the phone to enlist Stan's help. But Mick had asked that I keep this between the two of us. I leaned back and thought for a while. If Lina wasn't in the missing persons database, that had to mean she'd either been found, or that she'd never been reported as missing. Or, I realized, it could also mean she was dead.

I exited the database and started a new search. I typed, "Lina Ortiz kidnapped Tijuana" into the search bar. I scrolled down to view the recommended hits, but nothing looked right. I tried a broader search: "Americans kidnapped in Mexico, 1988." Once again, I perused the list of articles, but nothing was matching up. I sighed in frustration.

Outside, the rain had stopped. I could hear Mom and Harvey talking quietly. It was cute the way he walked her home each night. There was still no word on their official status, but Wanda and I had noticed that every morning and every evening ended with a long hug between the two. And for the twelve hours in between it was nonstop laughter and chatter, everywhere they went. At the end of the day, when Mom and I would return to the camper, it was always "Harvey this" and "Harvey that" until her head hit the pillow.

They were saying their final goodbyes now, so I closed my computer and put my notes away.

The following day was Trevor's memorial, and my last chance to see Stan for the next two weeks. Since he and Cinnamon were leaving for the K-9 training course directly from the twilight service, they came early to spend the day with us, while we did our rounds.

We were in the kitchen for the early afternoon shift. I was putting the finishing touches on two cheeseburgers and fries, while Stan scrubbed the dirty dishes from lunch. As I was leaving the kitchen to serve the customers, the dogs ran to the back screen door to look out. I could hear male voices coming from behind the café when I reentered the kitchen. One of the voices belonged to Harvey; the other, I didn't recognize. I inched toward the screen and peeked down the path. Harvey was coming toward us carrying a large cardboard box. The man next to him was in his early fifties. He was attractive, with a full head of blonde hair. He was outfitted in designer jeans, a nicely pressed button-up shirt, and a pair of loafers. The face was older, but recognizable. It was Tim.

I was just about to step out and greet them when I realized they were arguing. I glanced behind me, making sure there was no towering pyramid of pots and pans in my path. Then I carefully backed away from the door and listened up real close.

"I'm not having this discussion with you, Timothy," Harvey said sharply.

"We have to talk about it some time." Tim's voice tightened with frustration.

"And this is not that time."

I peered out from the recesses of the kitchen, as Harvey and Tim came into view. They approached the walk-in refrigerator, just outside the kitchen door. Harvey unlatched the sealed door and stepped inside with the box he was carrying.

Tim held the door open and said, "When will be the right time, then?"

"I don't know." Harvey's voice echoed from inside the cooler. "Perhaps some time when my men aren't turning up dead, or nearly dying from heart attacks."

"You know what, Dad? If I didn't know better, I'd think you care more about your employees than you do your own son."

Tim stepped back just as Harvey appeared in the opening. Harvey's arms hung by his sides. His face drooped with sadness. "Son…"

Tim plucked the sunglasses from his head and slid them over his eyes. He spun around and marched away. Over his shoulder he called, "You wouldn't have even found those beloved workers of yours, if it hadn't been for me."

# thirteen

The sun crept toward the horizon, draping its filtered light over Bear Springs like a soft, pink quilt. The birds hushed their singing. The river slowed its course. Serenity enveloped the land, as nightfall made its measured approach.

Harvey stood solemnly at the water's edge, with the cardboard box resting at his feet. His hands were clasped behind his back as he waited dutifully, like a reverend at the end of the wedding aisle on a hot summer day.

Stan, Mom, and I stood as a group, with Ranger and Cinnamon lying in the weeds beside us. Wanda, Nicole, and Colt made another cluster nearby. We were all facing Harvey, quietly waiting for the service to begin. Tim and Mick were the only two missing. After Tim's argument with his father that afternoon, I wasn't sure he'd bothered to stick around.

A burst of laughter caused us all to turn. The two stragglers were coming our way. Tim looked boisterous, bouncing down the trail with a can of beer in his hand. He appeared to be in the middle of a funny story, or perhaps a distasteful one, judging by the look of scorn on Mick's face. As Tim carried on, the others in our assembly began to glare at him like a theatre audience, shooting dirty looks to the noisy crowd behind them.

Mick stepped forward, bridging the narrow gap between the two small groups. Tim, who had reluctantly settled down, fell in line behind him, creating a back row for himself.

Ignoring his son's rude behavior, Harvey pressed his lips together in a subdued smile and then gave everyone a welcoming nod. In a rusty voice he said, "Thank you all for joining me."

He took a moment to clear his throat. Then he continued, speaking slowly and clearly.

"Trevor had a peculiar habit. Some of you may know about this, some may not. Every morning, before the sun broke over those mountains, he was here—at his fishing spot." Harvey paused and looked out toward us. "Rain or shine, Trevor started each day right where we're standing, with his line in the water."

A thoughtful smile crossed his face. "The only reason I knew about this, was that I'd see him walk by my cabin with his fishing pole every morning, while I was up doing my daily devotionals. I know from my own experience that waking at that hour takes dedication. And I became fascinated, watching this young man day after day. He wasn't religious, but he had devotion, you see. And so one day…I asked him about it." Harvey hesitated, as though to invoke the memory. "Trevor told me that he grew up in a trailer park with his mother and grandparents. They struggled financially, living on his grandfather's social security checks and his mother's waitressing salary. According to Trevor, the only thing he could truly count on as a child, was finding his grandfather at the river every morning with his fly rod. He said he once asked his grandpa about the daily ritual. Trevor said to me, 'Mr. Watts, my grandpa told me that you've got to have something to wake up for. Even if a man has no job, and no food in the cupboard… If he can find just one reason to get himself out of bed each morning, then eventually, he'll find success, too.'"

Harvey's voice had begun to break. He focused on the ground while the emotional swell passed. "Trevor stored up his grandfather's wisdom. And he faithfully lived it out, each and every day." Harvey fixed his aggrieved eyes on Tim. "What more can we as parents ask of our children?" He stopped once again, looked down, and shuffled his feet. "Trevor may have had some miles to go on his journey toward a happy, stable life. But his actions—something as simple as getting out of bed and going fishing every morn-ing—exemplified his strong will to overcome his struggles and to make a better future for himself. And I know…that if given the chance, he would have succeeded."

The sounds of sniffling were amplified in the gap of silence. Mom pulled out a travel pack of Kleenex and began passing tissues down the line.

Harvey redirected his attention to the rest of us. "Ac-cording to tradition, the perfect lifespan of man is 120 years. This…lofty goal…highlights the heart of the tragedy before us—the unfulfilled potential of a young soul." Harvey looked at the box resting at his feet. "That is why I've chosen to re-member this occasion by releasing these 97 gardenias into the river. Each flower representing one year of life which our friend deserved, but did not receive. I've divided the flowers into packs, which each person may disburse. As you step forward to receive your flowers, please take the opportunity to share a kind memory of Trevor, if you would like to do so. Please, whoever would like to go first…" Harvey stooped down and opened the box, expelling the intoxicating scent of gardenia blooms.

Without warning, Tim broke through from the back row, nearly knocking Wanda over as he bumped her shoulder with his. Harvey righted himself with a start and stumbled backward a step, as his son took center stage by storm. With a drunken sway, Tim raised his beer high in the air and jeered, "You were a better man than me, Trevor!" Then he swallowed the last gulp, crushed the can in his hand, and chucked it into the river. The crinkled Bud Light slapped the surface of the water and began wobbling its way over the ripples.

My first instinct was to yell, "Hey, that's littering!" But thankfully I said nothing. Instead, I joined the others, who stood slack-jawed, mesmerized by the aluminum ducky.

As Tim strode toward us to make his exit, we moved like a school of fish, giving him a wide passing lane. He strutted past and shouted, "You're welcome for the flowers, by the way. *Dad.*"

We glanced around, exchanging looks of shock. Harvey stared fiercely after his boy, with his lips tightening in a silent display of wrath. I peeked at my mother. She was observing Harvey with a troubled expression that reminded me of a stage mom, ready to aid her struggling actor the moment they looked her way.

When Tim had finally gone, Harvey took a deep breath. He relaxed his face, raised his eyebrows, and said, "Anyone else?"

I couldn't contain myself. I chuckled with compassion and said, "Oh, Harvey, we love you." Then I rushed toward him with open arms.

He hugged me back and humbly replied, "Thank you, dear." After a moment, he said, "Would you like to be first?"

"I'd love to." He handed me a small package containing the heads of ten white flowers. I gazed out toward my friends and family and smiled bravely while I tried to think of something to say. Stan returned a supportive smile. "I never got to meet Trevor," I began. "But I'm grateful to him for bringing us all closer as a family. So…love you guys." I gave Harvey another quick hug, and then proceeded toward the shore, where I kneeled and carefully set my gardenias adrift.

After I returned to my place, Wanda took her turn. She received her flowers and spun around to speak. Her eyeliner had become a thick smudge beneath her lower lids. In a shaky voice she said, "Trevor called me *Wandawg.* I never had a nickname before. I'm gonna miss that." She lowered her head momentarily, and then turned quickly and placed her flowers in the river.

Nicole moved forward, with a tissue in one hand. "Trevor was like an older brother to me." She stopped to wipe her nose. "He liked to pull pranks on me. Like when he got that bear costume, and he made growling noises outside my window one night." The crowd laughed softly. "But he was also kind to me. He always brought me a surprise, whenever he went to town for supplies." She looked at Harvey apologetically. "It was nothing extravagant. Just like, a candy bar or a magazine." Harvey smiled and nodded his approval. "And also, he was always there for me when I needed someone to listen." Her face tightened suddenly, and she began to whimper. "I'll never forget you, Trevor." She broke away with a sob and headed for the water.

The rest of the group came forward, one at a time. No one else had any words to share.

As the final trail of flowers voyaged toward the tip of the sun, we bowed our heads and paid our last respects by observing one minute of silence. When we opened our eyes, the sun had dipped out of view, and darkness was rushing in to take its place.

A warm hand slipped over mine and gave it a gentle squeeze. I turned my head toward Stan, whose gaze was directed at the ground in front of us. He pointed his finger. I looked down to see a white moon flower, opening its petals in plain view. Stan squeezed my hand again and pointed all around. "Oh my goodness!" I covered my mouth in awe.

My outcry startled the others, who jerked their heads in our direction. "The flowers," I exclaimed, "they're blooming!"

Up and down the riverbank, the glowing white beauties emerged from the dark fields, creating a mirror-like image of the night sky. The group fell silent, as each person bore witness to the hand of Providence. Faith aside, all our spirits were touched that night.

While the others returned to their cabins, Stan and Harvey walked Mom and me in the opposite direction, toward our place. "Harvey, that was an amazing memorial," I said.

"Magnificent," Mom echoed.

"Thank you very much," he replied. "It's sad to say, but I've had some practice." He continued a few more steps before adding, "You know, I did something similar for Jack."

"You did?" Mom said, with surprise.

"I did. It was a few months after he passed—when we came back up for the summer. Mom and I brought flowers from the shop and took them to the river, where he and

I used to swim when we were little." Harvey's shoulders dropped. He looked toward Mom with remorse in his eyes. "Ruth, I…I'm sorry I never contacted you. I wanted to. I wanted to send you flowers. And I thought of you and the girls often…" He stopped abruptly, as the emotion took hold of his voice.

Mom filled the gap. "It's all right, Harvey. Nothing was expected…"

"It's just that…I was conflicted," he interrupted. "I was torn between what I wanted, and what I knew Jack would have wanted." There was a long pause.

"I'm not sure I understand," Mom said cautiously. "I don't think Jack would have had a problem with you sending flowers, or staying in touch…"

Harvey shook his head and sighed. "I've probably said too much."

I got a funny feeling inside. "Does this have something to do with your surfing trip in Mexico?"

Harvey forced a laugh. "I have laid a nice trap for myself, haven't I?" Mom and I exchanged worried looks.

"If something happened there, and you two promised not to talk about it, it's okay. We would never ask you to betray Dad's confidence," I assured him.

"Thank you, Pepper. But no, it was nothing like that," he insisted. "Let me assure you, your father was a wonderful, upstanding man—even in his youth." Harvey interlaced his fingers and debated his next move. "What happened in Mexico between me and your father was just a simple disagreement."

"It doesn't sound so simple," I contended mildly.

"All right," he conceded with a heavy sigh. "I won't go into details, but, while we were on our vacation, I let your dad in on a family secret. It was something I felt should be exposed. But he was against my idea because he was afraid it would hurt too many people. I was angry at first. I wanted his support. We barely spoke for the rest of the trip. But in the end, I took his advice and never told a soul." He walked a few more paces before continuing. "Sometimes I regret my decision. Jack was always the type to run away from his problems, rather than face them head-on. Anyway…" he said, shaking his head, "I am the only person alive who knows the secret now. When I die, it will be buried with me."

❀ ❀ ❀

We reached the trailer and said our goodbyes. Stan promised to call often and to come see us as soon as he and Cinnamon returned from their training. Then he gave Harvey a lift home, on his way out of town.

Mom and I crawled into the camper, nearly collapsing onto the sofa. It had been a long day, with an emotional gauntlet at the finish line. There was so much to talk about, I hardly knew where to begin. "Any clues as to what this *Watts family secret* might be about?"

Mom laid her head back and closed her eyes. "Pepper, we don't need to go sticking our noses where they don't belong…"

"Harvey wanted to expose the truth. Now that everyone's dead, there's no one left to be hurt, right? Why shouldn't the man be able to unburden his soul?"

"It's not our business."

"He wants to talk about it, though. You can tell. We had him right at the precipice…"

"Honestly, Pepper."

"It's just a matter of time. And maybe with a little bit of encouragement…"

"I will not. And neither will you. Just leave it."

Ranger jumped onto the couch and lay down with his head on my lap. I petted him for a while, before switching topics. "How about that Tim? What a gem *he* turned out to be."

Mom groaned. "I was ready to strangle that kid. Showing up drunk, and disrespecting his father—who happens to be one of the most wonderful people in this world?"

"They had a big blowout before the memorial. I heard them arguing behind the café this afternoon."

"Yeah, Harvey told me about that."

"What did he say about it?"

Mom scowled. "You were there, Pepper. You would know better than I what took place."

"Well, it was difficult to hear everything. Not that I was trying to listen in or anything…"

Mom rolled her eyes at me. "Why don't I believe that?" she said, with a forced laugh. She continued, "Harvey said that Tim accused him of caring more about his employees than he did about his own son."

"That was the gist of it," I replied. "But there was more. Tim was badgering him about something, and Harvey said he didn't want to discuss it."

"Ah…"

I squinted my eyes at her suspiciously. "See? You know something. Give it up!"

"Well," she continued reluctantly, "there is a current disconnect between the two regarding finances."

"Oh really…"

"And the only reason I'm telling you this, is because Harvey told me that he's mentioned some of this to you already…about Tim being in over his head in debt, and now with the gambling stuff…"

"Right," I said, pretending I wasn't hearing about the gambling for the first time. "Tim's creditors are starting to come down hard on him. He's scared and desperate for cash."

"And he's looking for a bailout from Harvey?"

"He's looking for more than a bailout. He's pressuring him to sell Bear Springs and give him his inheritance in advance."

# fourteen

It was Tuesday morning, two days after the memorial service. I was anxious to tell Mick about my initial attempts at locating Lina. With everything that had been going on, Mick and I hadn't had a chance to talk for a few days. I was hoping to give him a call today, but as it turned out, in addition to having never owned a computer, Mick had never possessed a cell phone, either. Now that we were partnering on this secret project together, I was wishing we had more discreet ways to contact one another. Showing up at each other's houses everyday was a sure way to draw unwanted attention *and* start the rumor mill going. The last thing I needed was people thinking he and I were having a love affair.

Business was slow at the general store that morning, so I grabbed a pair of ninety-nine cent fingernail clippers off the doodads shelf and stood over the trash can to do a little maintenance. Asleep in his doggie bed behind the register, Ranger's ears twitched to the sound of my trimming. I've always been amazed at how our brains, both animal and human alike, can evaluate the ambient noises while we sleep, deciding which ones to let us doze through, and which ones warrant our full and immediate attention.

When I finished my fingers, I kicked off my right sandal and propped my heel on the corner of the Rubbermaid receptacle, ready to take a whack at my small toes. I was in an extremely precarious position when I heard footsteps on the front porch. My head turned without permission, causing me to lose my balance. The plastic tub shot out from under me like a bowling pin, and I was off, hopping wildly on one foot, like a human pogo-stick with busted springs. Ranger's brain must have interpreted the commotion as a wild buffalo stampede and had him evacuate the area immediately. I, on the other hand, was so focused on saving my own neck that I forgot all about the customer entering the store and did nothing to filter the loud hullabaloos that normally precede accidental death. Following several harrowing moments, however, I was able to brace myself on the counter, bringing my ordeal to an end before any bodily functions were lost. I breathed deeply and looked up to see Mick standing inside the door with a look of amusement on his face.

I panicked. "Holy cow! Did you feel that earthquake?"

"I sure did, Pepper," he said, with a sly grin. "You had the whole building shaking."

I averted my eyes as a shameful smile spread across my face. Mick strolled toward the checkout area, noting the tipped over trash bin and the clippers, which I had unknowingly placed on the counter. "You should really sit down to do your toes, though. Everyone knows that."

I laughed obligingly and snatched the nail clippers into my hand. "I'll be sure to remember that next time," I said, making a mental note to add GETTING HYGIENE TIPS FROM A CAVEMAN to my all-time worst moments list.

"I'm glad you're here," I told him. "I wanted to talk to you yesterday, but never got the chance."

"Were you able to find anything on Lina?" he asked hopefully.

"Nothing popped up on my initial search, but I barely scratched the surface. I did discover one interesting tidbit, though. She's not on the missing person's list, so that at least tells us something."

Mick smoothed his hand over his scruffy jaw. "She didn't just disappear into thin air."

"Right. And that's good news for us. Whatever happened to her came to some type of resolution. And if she's still out there, we should be able to find her. We just need to do more digging online."

"Sounds good."

"I'll be back at my trailer between three and five this afternoon. Come by, and I'll show you how to do some searches on my computer. If anybody asks, you can say we've become walking buddies." I gave him a wink.

Mick and I sat together in my dinette and got straight to work. I showed him some computer basics and let him take the wheel. I figured he'd have a much keener eye than I would, scouring the web for his missing girlfriend. The amount of information generated from a simple inquiry of "Lina Ortiz" was staggering. We scrolled and scrolled, ravenously devouring the pages in the beginning. But after we'd gone a spell without any reward, our optimism diminished the further down screen we ventured. We changed our search parameters several times, scrolling and clicking, our eyes desperately searching for a recognizable clue. But as the coffee pot drained, so did our morale. Before we knew it, two hours had whizzed past, and I was due back at the general store again.

Mick tossed a tennis ball to Ranger as we trudged up the road together. He was putting on a good face, but I knew he was terribly disappointed not to have found a single crumb on the trail. I felt terrible, like I'd misled him about how easy it was going to be to turn something up.

"You did well today, Mick."

He side-armed the ball up the middle of the road. "How's that?"

"You got in there, gained some new skills. And this is just the beginning. It may be several more days or even weeks until we find something that can lead us to her."

"If she's even alive." Ranger trotted back with the dirty ball in his mouth. Mick bent down and pried it out. "We have no idea what happened to her." He gave the ball a weak, underhanded toss. "For all we know, we're chasing a ghost. I appreciate your help, Pepper, but…"

"Hey, we aren't surrendering that easily. I'm no computer expert, but I'm sure there are a gazillion other things we could try. Everything these days is about social networking and locating old friends. We just need to invest more time, that's all. Please, don't give up on this." I could see the hopelessness on his face—he looked the same way I felt when we were searching for Trevor in the woods.

Up ahead, Harvey and Mom were leaving the cafe, heading our way. "Yeah, all right," he said, with his eyes up the road. "I got nothin' better to do anyway. Same time tomorrow then?"

"You bet."

Mick veered off, giving the older folks a wave as he continued toward his cabin. I walked ahead until I reached Mom and Harvey. When we stopped to chat, I could see that Harvey wasn't wearing his usual joyous smile.

"Pepper, when you get the chance, dear, would you mind getting onto the computer in my office and doing me a favor?"

"Sure, what is it?"

"I just got off the phone with the bank, and it seems our balance is lower than it should be. I wanted to check our credit card charges, but I know you recently switched us over to a paperless system, and…I haven't figured out how to access that yet. Do you think you could…"

"Right. No problem. Am I looking for anything in particular?"

"Just see if anything sticks out. There's probably a simple explanation. Maybe it's inflation," he chuckled nervously. "But…best to give things a once-over, just to be sure."

I was getting a rotten feeling in my gut. "I'll take a look," I said. "Give ya a call if I see anything."

We said goodbye and moved on to our next worksta-tions. Wanda had locked the store before she moved to the café a few minutes earlier. I pulled out my key, unlocked the door, and turned the sign to show that we were open again. Then I went immediately to the back and logged into the Bear Springs Visa account.

Ever since I arrived at camp, I'd been fighting a nagging sensation. I loved Harvey, and I admired the way he was raised to champion people from all walks of life. It was beau-tiful. And if everyone believed the best of one another and cared for others the way he'd been taught to do, our world would be a better place. For sure. But sometimes, I'll admit, his management style worried me sick. Especially with guys like Colt around. Sure, he'd been a polite, decent worker thus far. But what did we really know about him? I mean, who hires a kid with nothing but a rap sheet as a resume? And then immediately hands him a credit card and the keys to the company car? I hinted at my misgivings a time or two, but Harvey operated on the principle that the more trust you show someone, the more trustworthy they will become. I anxiously typed in the password and prayed he was right.

I started with the June statement. Trips to Costco and Lowe's accounted for most of the expenses. Colt had also filled up at the Shell station several times and taken a few trips to Taco Bell. I shook my head in bewilderment. Thirteen dollars for one person at Taco Bell? Last time I checked, a crunchy taco cost thirty-five cents. Geez, maybe Harvey was right. Food prices were becoming outrageous. Either that, or Colt was bootlegging chalupas.

I clicked the NEXT button, and the screen took me to the current month of July. It looked much the same, with one small exception. There were now several charges from 7-Eleven, all in the seventy-to-ninety-dollar range. Even for a girl who was obviously behind the times, that seemed a bit pricey for a Slurpee. I let my gaze flow over the screen, like a detective, waiting for her wall of yellow Post-it notes to cry out to her.

"Aha," I yapped to myself. I'm not sure how, but something drew my attention to the fact that there were no expenses from the Shell station on the July statement. I studied the screen. It didn't look like Colt had stopped anywhere for gas all month. That couldn't be. I thought for a moment, and then remembered that some 7-Elevens had gas pumps. Okay, so that explained that. Although…I went back to the

June statement. The average gas bill then was only $50. What was Colt spending the extra twenty-to-forty dollars on at the convenience store? Had he purposely switched from the Shell station to 7-Eleven to disguise hidden purchases?

I could hear the wild shrieks of overly stimulated children outside. When it sounded like someone turned the volume all the way up, I knew they'd gotten in. Without thinking, I unplugged the laptop and carried it over to the cash register with me. Three boys, aged four, six, and eight, by my best estimates, were chasing each other around the store, getting Ranger all wound up.

"Fellas, let's not run in here, all right?" I cast an irritated glance toward their father, who was digging through the live bait cooler, paying them no mind. I set the computer down and moved between the aisles to keep an eye on the little terrors. I found the young one in the snack section, unravelling a Bit-O-Honey—possibly the worst candy ever made. I let him stick it in his greedy little mouth and give it a good chomp. I figured we'd have a solid two-to-three minutes before he could pry those baby teeth apart and start making noise again.

I moved on to find the older two in the camping aisle, sword fighting one another with telescoping weenie skewers. "Hey, Dad," I sang out. "You may want to round up your swashbucklers before they poke an eye out."

Their father was now hunkered over the bobber bucket, clawing around for a red and white sphere of the perfect size. "Boys, be good," he called out with absolute disinterest.

I shook my head in disgust and ambled back to the register. I wasn't babysitting this schlub's kids for him.

A pile of night crawlers and fishing tackle was dumped in front of me. "We'll also need a large bag of ice and three bundles of firewood," he informed me. He reached for his wallet as the three brothers streaked behind him and shot out the door with merchandise in their hands.

I pursed my lips. "I'll add those squirt guns to your bill, as well."

"Perfect," he responded. I rang him up and hoped to never see him or his sticky-fingered hellions again.

I was even more testy than before when I reopened Harvey's computer to resume my investigation of Colt. If he had come up with a sneaky scheme to score himself some lottery tickets and cigarettes, what other types of devious ploys might he be capable of?

It made me sick to my stomach to consider the possibilities. A person like Harvey was the perfect prey for any lowlife looking to take advantage of someone. Colt had a key to the office, which not only gave him access to the computer and everything that was on it, but also to the file cabinets, where we kept the employee information and our guest registration sheets, which contained credit card information. Even if he wasn't stealing data for himself, he could be selling it to others. We weren't just talking misuse of funds anymore. Now we were looking at possible bank fraud, credit card fraud, identity theft, and who knew what else.

I was so angry, I wanted to kick a door in. Bear Springs could not survive any type of financial crisis. Harvey had not been exaggerating when he said the campground did not bring in much revenue. A couple weeks earlier, he had asked me to go over the budget with him, and I was left in a state of shock. The amount of money that was generated during the open season was barely enough to cover our annual expenses, which included feeding and housing the staff.

I would not stand by and watch our campground go under. I got out my phone and dialed Harvey immediately.

"Pepper, I was just about to call you. Listen, don't worry about looking at the credit card charges. Your mother reminded me that I had taken some money out to help with Mick's medical costs. I'm not sure how I overlooked that."

I was so stunned, I didn't know what to say. I shook my head and crinkled my brow, trying to formulate words in my head. "Are you sure?" I asked. Fifteen seconds earlier, I was ready to ram through doors and knock heads together. "You're saying there's no money missing?"

"We're all square," he responded. I was still feeling utterly confused. I'd been sure I was on to something. Had I only seen what I wanted to see? Something that wasn't even there? "Forgive me, Pepper. I started right in on you and never let you speak. What was it you called me for?"

"Oh, uh…I guess it's nothing," I stammered. "I'm glad you got that resolved."

I was a bit jittery after we hung up. It was disturbing to realize how quick I'd been to jump to conclusions and allow myself to get so close to unleashing havoc on someone without any clear evidence. I walked to the refrigerated section and pulled a sparkling water from the shelf, hoping it would cool me down and clear my head.

As I returned to the register, I took a swig and chuckled at the irony of what I'd just done. Instead of going immediately to the office to sign out my drink, I decided to try to remember to do it later, knowing full-well I would probably forget. Harvey wouldn't make a fuss over one drink, I had told myself. I smiled and shook my head in amazement. Perhaps Colt was taking advantage of the system here and there, but I guess we all did, in our own ways. I'm sure Harvey was aware of that fact, too. And he still placed his trust in us. I suppose that's what folks call *grace*.

I jostled the mouse to wake the computer and logged out of the Visa account. The homescreen stared at me. Since I had the computer out, maybe I'd do a little more detective work for Mick. I clicked on a search engine and resumed the quest for Lina.

A half-hour into my hunt, I landed on an article which had appeared ten years earlier in *Woman's World Magazine*. It was titled, "From Abductee to Healer: A Trauma Specialist Opens Up About Her Own Journey After 25 Years of Silence."

I clicked on it, just out of sheer interest. The article began,

*Dr. Caroline Thompson lifts herself from the pearl-colored leather. Her absence reveals the elegantly scalloped back of a twin-seat sofa, which has been thoughtfully positioned just beyond the reach of the afternoon sun. The Seattle Harbor blazes ten stories below, each glint of sunlight appearing like a tongue of fire on the falling crests.*

*Dr. Thompson quietly approaches a panel on the wall, and with a light touch, flips a switch. The bright glare suddenly softens, as the floor-to-ceiling windows fade from clear to frost. A calming sense of anonymity soothes the air, a slightly more subtle effect of the electronic window film.*

*Having offered up her chaise lounge, the psychologist resumes her position on the couch, a space normally occupied by her patients. The intentional seating arrangement does not go unnoticed.*

*At first, her story is unrelatable. It is too much of a struggle to place this refined woman in such a broken world. But her words are persuasive. With articulate expression, she speaks of growing up in poverty and being the only child raised by her single mother—her five older siblings having been taken into foster care years before she was born, due to alcohol and drug use in the home. It is a sad story, not unfamiliar to many Americans.*

*In order to escape the unhealthy and oftentimes abusive conditions, Dr. Thompson dropped out of school and left home at the age of fifteen. She spent the next several years working at fast food chains and living with friends. Though she desired a better future for herself, she felt as though she were blocked in on all sides, destined to follow the same path as her mother. Then the unimaginable happened.*

DR. THOMPSON: *When I was eighteen, I drove to Mexico with a group of friends to go drinking. We were just going to stay a few hours and then come back home. As we were leaving the night club to return to our car, I somehow got separated from everyone else. Before I knew it, I was grabbed from behind and thrown into a van. As the van pulled away, I was blindfolded and gagged with dirty rags. The smell and taste of those rags was so revolting. It was like a musty motor oil blend. Still very vivid. I was driven to a home and locked in a room.*

INTERVIEWER: *What can you tell us about the place where you were held?*

DR. THOMPSON: *I remember it being dark, even during the daylight hours. There were no windows. A small amount of light seeped in through the crack under the door, but that was all. The only piece of furniture in the room was a heavily soiled mattress, which sat on the gritty floor. It reeked of old urine. The odors were very impacting. I didn't know it at the time, but I was newly pregnant then, and as a result, my sense of smell was heightened.*

*INTERVIEWER: How were you treated during your captivity?*

*DR. THOMPSON: My abductors left me alone for the most part. I was given food and water. I was physically unharmed. Psychologically, however, I was in grave danger. The level of fear and uncertainty that one experiences in that type of situation can cause irreparable damage to the brain.*

*INTERVIEWER: Were you ever made aware of the intentions of your kidnappers?*

*DR. THOMPSON: Yes. After I was rescued, the Mexican police informed me that my kidnapping had been orchestrated by a gang of teenagers, who were hoping to impress the local drug lord. Apparently, they hatched this impulsive plan to snatch an American off the street and then offer him or her to the drug cartel in return for an eventual cut of the ransom money. But the cartel was not swayed. They wanted nothing to do with the amateurs and their shoddy work. And rightfully so, as it turned out. After they captured me, the teens were so proud of what they'd done, they began bragging about the "gringa" that they stole. Word quickly spread to the local police, and three days after my abduction, I was saved.*

*INTERVIEWER: What do you remember about the rescue?*

*DR. THOMPSON: It was very quick. I heard a lot of noise as they raided the home. Then the door opened, and someone ushered me through the house and into the back of a squad car. They drove me straight to the border, where they basically washed their hands of me. It was quite a surreal experience. I knew I'd been through something colossal. I could have easily been killed or raped. But there I was, dropped at the bus stop, essentially being told to just go on as if nothing happened. And believe me, I was tempted to try. But something inside urged me to get help. So that's what I did. Instead of going back home, I walked to the nearest pay phone and got in touch with my aunt, who worked as a family counselor. She hired a taxi to pick me up and drive me to her home, where she took me in and quite literally changed the course of my life. It was shortly thereafter that we discovered I was pregnant with my first daughter. While I waited for her to be born, I earned my GED. My aunt was so impressed with my level of aptitude that she encouraged me to continue my studies after my daughter's birth. Under her care and support, I went on to earn my bachelor's degree, and eventually, my PhD...*

Before I could finish the article, my attention was hijacked to the bottom of the screen, where the top of a photo peeked out. My hand shook as I scrolled down to view the picture in its entirety. With my eyes darting hungrily around the image, I took in the information quickly. It was a family of five posing on a pier, with a large sailboat named "Tied to the Doc" immediately behind them. In the front row, a boy aged twelve or thirteen sat cross legged. Kneeling beside him were his two older sisters, one in her mid-teens, the other in her mid-twenties. The children were all gorgeous, with bright white smiles and skin bronzed by the sun. Caroline Thompson and her husband stood proudly behind them with their arms wrapped lovingly around one another.

A tingling sensation spread across the back of my neck. I enlarged the photo and gazed at the debonaire Hispanic woman. Then I ran out the door.

# fifteen

Mick and I raced back to the store together. I tapped the keyboard and waited for the photo to reappear. When it did, a clear look of recognition flashed across his face. I backed away, giving Mick space to absorb the impact. With his eyes fixed on the screen, he cradled his head with his hands, as though he were trying to keep himself held together. His lips began to shudder. "She looks happy," he said, as the tears soaked his cheeks.

I moved closer and put a hand on his back. "I believe she is happy, Mick. She's an amazing woman."

He pulled his eyes from the photo and turned to me. "I can't believe you found her. Thank you, Pepper. You have no idea what it means, just to see her face. And to know…" Mick's voice broke.

I stepped forward and bound him in a bear hug. Then I gently eased away and said, "You should read the article. Why don't you take Harvey's computer to the office, where you can have some privacy, huh?"

He nodded. "Yeah, okay." He held the laptop in front of him as he walked to the back room. I watched him from behind, as his eyes continued to pore over the snapshot of his Carolina Ortiz, and as he would soon discover, the beautiful daughter they shared.

As soon as the door clicked shut behind him, I began to pace around the store. I was so happy for Mick and the relief he must now be feeling. And even more so, I was elated over the fact that he was a father. I couldn't wait to see his reaction to the news.

I tried to sound occupied out in the storeroom, as though I were busily tidying up while Mick read through the article. In reality, my ears were trained on that office door like an owl to a fat field mouse. I held my breath in spurts, anticipating a gasp or a light snivel, or even the grainy sound of tissue being pulled from the box. But I was getting zero feedback.

I stayed away, giving Mick sufficient time to read the article twice through, if that was what he needed. Then I couldn't stand it any longer. I knocked daintily and called out his name. He emitted a short grunt, which I took as my invitation to enter. I pushed the door open, revealing Mick's still profile, seated in front of the desk. The scene reminded me of one of those spooky cinematic moments, where the secretary approaches her boss in his office chair and spins him around, only to discover the fatal gunshot wound oozing from his Joseph A. Bank dress shirt.

I hunched over, drawing my clenched fists toward my chest. "Mick? Are you all right?" He remained frozen in place. I leaned around his body—no blood. "Hey," I gently appealed. "Talk to me."

At last, he twirled to face me. His face was pallid, and small sweat beads were forming below his hairline. I cleared the worried look from my face and replaced it with an encouraging smile. "It's good, isn't it? It's all wonderful news."

Mick wiped the moisture from his forehead. He took a ragged breath and shook his head. "I don't know. I'm not sure what to think. It's not what I expected." He leaned back in the chair and put his hand over his mouth.

"It's all right. You're in shock. It's totally understandable."

He leaned forward and pointed to the screen, which displayed the family photo. "Is that my daughter?" I could see the torrent of emotions, tossing him about.

"What do you think?" I asked.

"I mean, yeah. Lina and I were together for almost a year. I can't imagine she would have been with anyone else." A perfectly formed teardrop began to slide from the corner of his eye. He smudged it away with a knuckle and maintained his composure.

"She's beautiful. Probably in her mid-thirties by now. May even have a family of her own…"

Mick let out an exasperated laugh. "It's too much! I was ready to handle whatever we found out about Lina. I was even preparing myself to reach out to her, if she turned out to be okay. But now this? This changes everything, Pepper, can't you see that?" I didn't answer. "I abandoned *two* people. My own daughter!" Tears of frustration spilled into his lap. "What must Lina think of me, huh? What a man I turned out to be."

I heard the jingle of the front door. "I'll be right back." Ranger stayed behind to comfort Mick, while I sold a matching pair of inner tubes. By the time I returned, he had calmed down a bit.

"And who knows what Lina told the girl about me?" he continued, as though I had never left. "What if she lied, and made up some story? I can't come waltzing back into their lives now, turning everything upside down on them. Look how content they are."

I nodded. He was right. Things were more complicated now, with a child involved. "Try not to jump to conclusions," I advised. "I don't get the sense from the article that Lina is holding any grudges against you. If anything, that experience made her who she is today."

"That's just it though, Pepper. She never even mentioned me. She changed the whole story to cut me out of it. There was no mention of the fight, nothing!"

"She might have been doing that to protect you guys."

Mick's face blushed. "If she cared so much, why didn't she call me to tell me she was all right?"

"Would you have picked up if she had?"

Mick stood and squeezed past me. I expelled a heavy sigh and watched him exit the building.

The hardest thing about the whole Mick situation was having to keep a lid on it. When Mom joined me in the camper that night, it was all I could do not to go into an immediate blabbing tirade. I needed some sort of outlet. Thankfully, before any promises were broken, Mom introduced an attention-grabbing topic of her own.

Seated on the couch, she said, "I'm a little worried about Harvey."

"Oh?" I looked over my shoulder before closing the refrigerator door with my elbow. I stepped across the walkway and handed mom a Perrier before plopping down beside her. I gently untwisted my own cap, adeptly controlling the release of pressure. One of my few talents.

"It's the money stuff. I don't know if he's just got too much on his mind, or if he's starting to lose track of things…"

I squinted in confusion. "What money stuff? You mean the bank account thing from today?"

"Mm-hmm." Mom held the plastic green bottle in her lap, still unopened.

"I thought we settled that. The money went toward Mick's hospital bills."

"That's what he said—originally. But then later today, he admitted we were still short, even after taking Mick's bills into account."

I sat forward with concern. "How much are we talking?"

"He thinks maybe four or five thousand?"

"What?" A wave of nausea passed over me. I leaned over my lap and closed my eyes. When I opened them again, I jumped up and began pacing back and forth. "We're going to have to tighten things up around here," I said sternly. "And for starters, I don't think every Tom, Dick, and Harry on staff here needs their own set of keys to the city. At least not to the office. There's way too much sensitive information lying around in there."

"You think someone is stealing?" Mom's eyes grew large. "Is it Colt?"

I shrugged. "No one is above suspicion here. Harvey makes it too easy for people. He takes in desperate folks and then gives them all this rope to hang themselves with. It's practically entrapment!"

"Oh, Pepper, you don't really believe that. I think we could all do with a little more faith in our fellow man."

"See? Harvey's got you trained. You sound just like him," I said resentfully. "And since you mentioned it, yes, I did come across some suspicious activity on the credit card this afternoon. It doesn't add up to five thousand dollars, not even close. But it does make me wonder what we might find if we started poking around a little bit more."

"Oh, no."

"Yeah." I put my hands on my hips. "We should be keeping our eyes on Colt."

Ranger jumped out of his plush bed and ran to the door. I walked over to look. Two beams of yellow light cut across our view, as the sound of a large diesel engine droned louder. The lights rotated ninety degrees until they shot through the screen door, rendering me blind. I reached up to shield my eyes and shrieked, "Who the heck is this?" Sensing my alarm, Ranger let out an unnerving growl. When I looked down at him, the fur between his shoulder blades was protruding like a patch of spiny quills.

The engine sputtered to a stop, and the lights were cut. I opened the door to let Ranger out before stepping outside myself. Mom followed behind. The three of us inched closer to the front of a large truck. We all flinched when the driver door suddenly flew open.

A husky female voice filled the air. "Relax, ladies, it's just me. Oh my blinking heck, I thought that winding road was never going to end! It took me way longer to get here than it should have. Well, I have much to catch you up on. You're never going to believe what that dirtbag did to me. Oh here, Pepper? Take my shoes, please. I'll bust a heel if I try to jump outta this truck with them on. Thank you, honey." A pair of navy-blue high heels were thrust out of the opening, with two fingers hooked around the heel straps.

Mom and I stood speechless, staring at the dangling shoes.

"Mother? Am I hallucinating?"

"No, dear."

"Piper's here?"

"Mm-hmm."

"And she came in a tow truck?"

"Looks like it."

"And you're sure this isn't a dream?"

"I'm fairly certain it's real."

"Crap." I trudged forward and obediently reached out for the shoes, already feeling manipulated.

Piper climbed out carefully, with a matching blue purse in the crook of her arm. I'm not sure if Ranger remembered her from his early days, but something inside him decided she was no longer a threat and needed a specially warm welcome. Before her last painted piggy touched the ground, he was all over her, giving her the treatment we'd come to call "The Deluxe Dog Wash."

Piper squealed and waved her arms frantically. "No! Get down! Ow, it's stepping on me. Somebody get this thing off me!"

I watched with pleasure as my barefooted sister twirled in circles with her poor-mannered partner, who couldn't keep his paws off her. It looked like they were doing the Redneck Waltz. Poetry in motion, if you asked me. Mom finally stepped in, taking Ranger by the collar. Piper gaped at her outfit, like a Homecoming Queen who'd just had a glass of punch thrown on her gown.

"You remember Ranger, don't you?" I smiled triumphantly and ignored my mother's sideways glances.

Mom frowned with concern. "Piper, what's happened?"

My sister snatched her shoes from me and steadied herself against the side of the truck, while she pulled the straps over her heels with impressive speed and coordination. "C'mon, ladies, let's get inside. I'm in desperate need of a drink. And then I'll tell you the whole sordid tale."

"Sorry, Pipe, I don't have any alcohol."

She thrust a pointer finger in the air as she paraded past me, leading the way toward my RV. "I brought my own. It's packed in the suitcases. Do you mind bringing those in, Pepper?" Before I could even answer, she had vanished into the trailer, with Mom and Ranger tagging close behind. "I thought Pepper said she could sleep eight in here?" I heard her say.

I mumbled a light obscenity under my breath and trudged ahead. Piper could get her own dang bags.

❊ ❊ ❊

A few minutes later, Mom and I settled on the couch while my sister stood before us sipping her homemade cocktail, steadying her nerves before she began. I felt like we were sitting in the front row at the black box theatre, waiting for the lights to dim.

"So," she opened, with her eyes fixed on the ceiling, head bobbing slightly. "As you may have guessed, I have left Scotty." Her head flopped forward. She covered her eyes, careful not to smudge the makeup. "Oh poop, I swore I wouldn't cry!" She paused for effect before removing her hand and looking out toward the audience. Piper's eyeballs were as dry as the desert sand. I'd seen better stage acting from the Montessori nursery kids.

"Never in a million years did I think things would end this way between us," she continued theatrically.

"Just tell us what he did," Mom said curtly, cutting through all the melodrama.

"No problem," Piper answered, effortlessly shifting from Scarlett O'Hara to Mary Jo Buttafuoco. "I caught the slime-ball out in the parking lot, hugging the new part-time driver this morning. I knew he was messin' around with her! He's obsessed with the little tramp, cuz she's a *roller derby chick.* Like that makes a woman attractive in any way, shape, or form!" Piper shook her head in disgust. "I coulda kept my ladies and gotten a pair of roller skates, instead!" She began to laugh maniacally. And then actual tears appeared. They mixed with her mascara and left her face streaked, like an abandoned watercolor canvas. Mom and I stayed glued to our seats, finally getting our money's worth.

"He was so obvious about it, too," she continued, as the anger resurfaced. "Ever since he hired her, he hasn't been able to stop yappin' about the stupid roller derby. Even dragged me out on a Friday night to watch one of her dumb matches—er, I mean, *bouts.* Pardon me. And…the schmuck had the nerve to call it a date!" She took a gulp of her drink and swallowed hard. "You wanna know the funny part?" She continued without waiting for a reply. "Her name is Saya. Can you guess what her derby name is? *SAYANARA!*" She cackled hysterically and then raised her drink in a toast. "Yep. Sayanara, baby! I hope she was worth it." Piper tipped her head back and emptied the glass.

# sixteen

I woke up the next morning feeling groggy and irritable. My entire night of sleep had been ruined by the rumbling sound of a whole-house generator, coming from my living room. I stepped into my slippers and threw open the bedroom door, making the vibrations even louder. I could see Mom in the kitchen, taking her morning pills. I stomped toward her, waving my hands to get her attention over all the noise. She finally looked my way and waved back. Across the aisle, Piper was turned away from us, slumbering peacefully on the sleeper sofa.

I threw my hands in the air. "What is that?" I yelled.

Mom swallowed another pill and answered, "The noise?"

"Yes," I answered with vexation. "Why does it sound like the motocross in here?"

"It's Piper's CPAP."

"Her what?" I put a hand on my hip.

Mom raised her voice a notch. "Her machine that helps her get a good night of sleep."

My chin dipped as my eyebrows arched to their max. "Excuse me?" I spun around and stamped my padded feet to my sister's bedside. "Oh, heck no," I said, fumbling around for the cord. As soon as my fingers curled around that power cable, I gave it a firm yank, ripping it straight from the wall.

Having killed the racket, I glanced down at my sleeping sister. I hadn't seen her without makeup since we were kids. I leaned closer out of morbid curiosity. Her unrecognizable face was trapped beneath some kind of swamp creature breathing apparatus.

Her eyes fluttered open. A Kathy Bates body double was hovered over her, with a plug protruding from her balled fist. Piper shot straight up, and we both screamed.

She slapped a hand over her chest. "Pepper!" she shouted into her mask. "You scared the crap outta me!"

"You scared the crap outta *me*!" I volleyed back.

"Why did you turn off my CPAP?"

"Cuz it was driving me crazy! And Mom and I are trying to get ready for work!"

Piper threw the covers off her feet and twisted around to disconnect the end of her tube from the machine. "Move. I gotta pee." She crossed in front of me with a three-foot hose dangling from her plastic snout. I stood back and observed the bizarre demonstration. The tube swayed side to side like a shriveled elephant trunk as she loped toward the bathroom.

Mom moved in next to me. "You shouldn't crinkle your nose like that, Pepper. You'll get wrinkles."

I whispered back. "How long is she planning to stay?" Mom shrugged her shoulders in silence. Our stares were fixed on the bathroom door. "I say we give her a day and then put her to work."

Mom raised her brows and nodded in accord. "Kitchen?" she murmured out of the side of her mouth.

I turned my head to face her. "Dishes," I mouthed firmly.

Mom and I covered our giggles and broke away from each other, just as we heard the flush.

❀ ❀ ❀

Two hours later, I was working the register at the store, when Mick dropped in. Piper's sudden invasion had made me forget all about the Lina ordeal. He moved slowly, avoiding eye contact until he stood across the counter from me.

"Look, I'm sorry for running out on you yesterday. I was overwhelmed. Needed time alone to think things through."

I waved off his apology. "Totally understandable." I shifted my feet and waited for more.

"Thing is…knowing Lina's okay isn't enough. I realized that last night. I need to tell her I'm sorry, and that…I'd give anything for the chance to go back and do things differently."

"You've decided to contact her?"

He sighed heavily. "Yeah. I'm ready. I want to get this done. Do you think you could help me find a number for her?"

"Shouldn't be hard." I pulled out my smart phone and typed in her name, city, and profession. "This is it." I jotted the number onto a piece of scrap paper and passed it to him.

He took the paper and stared at the number.

"I'll be thinking about you," I said, feeling empathetic butterflies.

"Thanks," he replied softly. "I couldn't have done any of this without you."

I looked him in the eye. "I'm proud of you, Mick. I hope you realize that what you're doing takes extraordinary courage."

He pressed his lips together and formed a half-smile. "If shaking in your boots counts as courage…"

A customer entered the store. Mick gestured and said, "I'm gonna use the office phone." Then he disappeared down the aisle and closed himself in the room.

A gentleman in fishing apparel approached the counter and asked, "Do you have a lost and found here? I seem to have misplaced my sunglasses."

I bent down and slid the plastic tub into view. I rummaged for a moment. "No, I'm sorry—unless you're the owner of the pink Princess Jasmine shades…"

"Afraid not," he said, in no mood for joking. "These were polarized fishing lenses. Expensive, too." He ran a hand through his hair. "Maybe they'll turn up. I'll check back later." He started to leave and then spun around. "Oh! Wife asked me to get sodas while I'm here. She's steamed at me—apparently, I forgot to pack her wine coolers. I could have sworn I put them in the truck…"

As he fetched a six-pack of Dr. Pepper, I recalled the other camper who had come in earlier that morning to report a missing pocketknife. I was starting to get a sinking feeling inside.

I completed the sales transaction just as Mick emerged from the office. I took one look at him and knew something had gone terribly wrong. Mick stumbled toward me in a daze, looking like he was going to vomit. I rushed to him and immediately ushered him back into the office, where he could sit. He dropped into the chair and put his head between his knees. I stood over him, steeped in worry.

I tried to hide the panic in my voice as I begged him to talk. "Mick, can you tell me what happened?" I could hear him trying to calm himself as he breathed in through his nose and out through his mouth. I put a hand on his back, hoping the touch would stimulate him to return to an upright position.

He remained bent over and began rocking himself. "I dialed the number. A receptionist answered. I asked to speak to Dr. Thompson. She asked what it was regarding, and I said it was a personal matter. I could tell she was nervous, but she patched me through. Then a man picked up. I asked for Dr. Thompson, and he said, 'Speaking.' I told him I was looking for Caroline Thompson, and he paused." Mick's voice began to wobble. "He told me that Caroline Thompson had passed away—two years ago." Mick's back became spotted with perspiration. He fought through the tears and kept talking. "He asked if there was something he could help me with, and I said no, that I was just a friend from a long way back."

I shook my head in disbelief. "Oh Mick, I am so sorry..."

Harvey's landline rang. Mick jolted upright. "I'll get it," I volunteered. I reached across the desk and pulled the receiver to my ear. "Bear Springs Campground, how may I help you?" Mick leaned back, watching my face with troubled interest.

A male voice replied, "Hello, I believe Mick just called me from this number? Is it possible for me to speak with him again?"

My heart skipped a beat. "May I ask who's calling?"

"This is Dr. Jerry Thompson."

My jaw fell open. "Just a moment, and I'll let him know." I cupped the mouthpiece with my hand. "It's him! It's Dr. Thompson," I panted in a raspy whisper.

Mick's face tightened. He sat up straight and reached for the handset. "Hello?"

"Is this Mick Davis?" Dr. Thompson's voice carried through the headset, just loud enough for me to hear.

Mick frowned with confusion. "Yes, it is, but…how did you get my name?"

"I'm sorry. I'm afraid I have a bit of explaining to do. Caroline was my wife and business partner. After she got sick, she told me you might come looking for her one day. I know this is all strange, but she had something for you. And she made me promise to pass it along, if you ever surfaced. When you and I hung up just now, something in my gut told me it was you. I took a chance and hit the redial button." Mick was shocked into silence. "Mick, are you there?"

"I'm here," he replied weakly. "She…she has something for me?"

"Yes, and I would like to send it to you if you would provide me with a mailing address. I've not seen the contents of the envelope. Caroline sealed it and asked me to safeguard it until you came. But I know it meant a lot to her. It was one of her last dying wishes."

❈ ❈ ❈

That evening I made a fire. Mom, Piper, and I placed lawn chairs in a semi-circle around the crackling pit. We parked ourselves next to one another and sipped hot cocoa under the stars. I'm sure studies have been done about the science behind fireside gatherings. Whether it's the release of negative ions that makes them so pleasurable, or the primordial psychological boost that one gains by uniting forces and sheltering together. Whatever the case, it was nice. Piper's phone, which had been blowing up all day with texts and attempted calls from Scotty, was now switched off. Not a mention was made of current problems or worries. Instead, we recalled the happy times—the stories of growing up, of holidays and family trips to Bear Springs. We talked about Daddy, too. Yes, the Rose women built a little team camaraderie that night. And happily, we didn't have to step foot in any ladies' locker room to do it.

When the firewood had reduced to embers and ash, the conversation slowed. It was after ten o'clock, which under campground rules began the quiet hours. There were still a few kids running about. Their symphony of untamed noises could be heard from a distance.

I trained my camp host ear, hoping the conquest was nearly through. But instead of dying out, the disturbances grew steadily louder. The band of wild children were drawing near.

A moment later, we nearly leapt out of our chairs. Swishing sounds in the bushes behind us preceded a full-on attack, as a half-dozen boys hurdled through my camp, each one brandishing a burning stick.

Ranger jumped up to give friendly chase, evoking an elevated fit of screams and laughter. The mini marauders moved through quickly, hit the dirt road, and turned out of sight. I followed them loosely, smudging out the pieces of charred branches, which trailed behind them like glow-in-the-dark crumbs. I hollered for some assistance, knowing one stray ember in this environment could be disastrous. Mom and Piper spread out, combing the ground for cinders and signs of smoke. Ranger gave up his pursuit and returned to me, exuberated over his late-night escapade. We continued along the loop at a brisk pace, hoping to track down the miscreants and give them a little "come to Smokey" talk.

By now the noise had ceased. I passed by campsite after campsite, with no signs of the children. They must have skittered back to their tents to hide when they realized the management was after them.

Most of the sites were dark, barring the occasional silhouette inside a glowing dome. As Ranger and I rounded the curve, I spotted a large, multi-room tent. One end was lit by a lantern, revealing shadows that crossed back and forth. From the dark side of the tent came sounds of a shushing mother, trying to convince her crying toddler that he was exhausted and needed to go nighty-night. Outside, Dad was enjoying his solitude as he puffed on a fat cigar and loaded more wood onto the fire. I took a few more steps and brought the scene into focus. Leaning against the metal rim of the fire ring were three sticks—with charcoaled tips.

"Evening," I said, as I drew near.

The man squinted and gave his stogie a drag. He climbed into his reclining beach chair with a light grunt. "It's the lady from the general store. Let me guess, you're missing a gum ball?" A dry laugh escaped from his throat. He leaned his head back and tightened his lips for another suck.

I chuckled back, unamused, but pleased to know who I was dealing with. "Ah yes, the fisherman with three boys." I settled my eyes on the sticks.

"Four boys," he corrected.

"Huh." I cocked my head. "Must be a handful."

He crossed his ankles and joined his hands behind his head. "Just passing by, were you?"

"Afraid not. I need to have a talk with your sons about respecting the campground rules."

He snorted. "That's ridiculous. My kids are in the tent for the night."

"And three minutes ago, they were running through other people's campsites, screaming, hollering, and wielding burning sticks."

"If you haven't noticed, there are children crawling all over the place here. I don't see how you could possibly single out my family. In any case, it sounds like boys being boys. It's all harmless fun."

"They were disturbing guests who were trying to sleep. And they could have started a serious fire."

Three perfectly formed smoke rings wafted over his head. "I don't hear anyone running around now, and I don't see anything going up in flames, so…I'm not quite sure why you're standing here, disturbing *my* peace."

I wished I had a bucket of ice water to extinguish this guy and his dirty habit. "Consider it a warning," I said, with a clenched jaw. "First and last." I gave him one final stare and then turned to leave.

"Hey, lady," he called after me. "You don't intimidate me."

I stopped on a dime and spun around to face him. "Control your kids. Or I'll be back, and you won't like it."

Ranger and I turned up the road. As soon as we crossed into the darkness, my mom and sister stepped out of their hiding spots. Piper was ready to rumble.

"What a jackass!" she spewed. "I don't know how you kept your cool, Pep. I was seriously about to haul outta these bushes like freakin' Rambo."

We trooped toward home, three-across. "I wouldn't have stopped you," I replied. "This was my second run-in with him and his horrendous children. I swear, if I hear so much as a squirrel chirping a complaint against them, that family is outta here."

The tail-end of Piper's tow truck came into view. Just beyond that, a large shadowy figure moved toward us. I peered through the darkness, expecting recognition to kick in at any moment. Most guests became familiar faces after a day or two. But I was pretty sure I'd never seen this guy before.

Mom kindly offered a "good evening" as the scruffy man approached. He didn't reply. Instead, he turned his head away as he passed by. The odd behavior caught us all by surprise. We held our comments until we reached the camper.

As soon as we'd closed the door behind us, Piper spoke out. "I realize I'm a woman scorned, but am I the only one that got bad vibes from that guy just now?" Mom and I both shook our heads slowly.

"Where was he coming from?" Mom asked. "Everything up that way is closed for the night."

"Maybe he's just out on a walk." My voice was heavy with doubt.

"Without a flashlight?" Piper puckered her lips and shook her head. "And what was with all those heavy winter clothes he was wearing? That can't be good for his hygiene."

I stared out the kitchen window, deep in thought. An old nervous habit kicked in, forcing my fingertips toward my lips.

I hadn't taken a single nibble before Piper burst out, "Oh my gosh, Pepper! You still chew your nails? Grody!"

I brought my hand down quickly and frowned. As I spun around to face them, I drew a deep breath and exhaled forcefully. "I guess this would be a good time to tell you guys…"

"Tell us what?" they blurted out together.

"I think there's a thief at Bear Springs."

Unlike Piper, who retracted with surprise, Mom turned pensive. "What makes you think so?" she asked.

"A couple different people came in to check the lost-and-found box today. They were looking for small items— sunglasses, a pocketknife, that sort of thing. I was hoping they had just misplaced them, but now…"

Mom clasped her hands together. "Harvey and I had a woman stop by the RV today, asking if anyone's cars had been looted. She wasn't sure, but she said it looked like someone had been digging in her glovebox."

My heart began to thud. "Guys, I think we'd better go by the store and make sure there wasn't a break-in."

"Should we call Harvey?" Mom asked.

"No, I hate to disturb him. Let's just run up there and take a quick peek."

Armed with flashlights, we reentered the dark night. The chill in the air hit our faces like a splash of water, reviving our senses. As we walked, Mom recalled the issue of the missing funds. We debated whether the same perpetrator could be responsible for everything that was going on. Once again, Colt's name was thrown around.

The store was dark. I unlocked the door and flipped on the lights. At first glance, everything seemed in order. I checked behind the counter and verified that the cash register was undisturbed. Then I dashed to the office. With a separate key, I unlocked that door and flicked the switch. Ranger pushed his way in ahead of me, ever mindful of the bottomless box of biscuits, which sat on Harvey's desk. Mom and Piper stayed back, hovering around the entrance to the office while I poked around inside.

The file cabinets were closed, the computer monitor was dark. In the small closet, I reached into the hiding spot where Harvey kept the petty cash box. We never had much paper money on hand, since most of customers paid with plastic. Nevertheless, I'd been on him recently to invest in a legitimate safe that someone couldn't easily stuff in their jacket and walk away with. I pulled the steel box out and opened it to verify the contents. And then I heard the bells on the front door jingle.

I stood up straight and listened with alarm. My mom and sister were frozen in place, with looks of panic on their faces. "Get in here you two, quick!" Mom and Piper shoved their way into the tiny room with me and Ranger. "Lock the door and turn off the light," I whispered. Everything went black. I crouched in a defensive position and tuned in to the sounds of footsteps, working their way across the storeroom. "Everybody stay quiet," I hissed from behind.

A shadow appeared in the crack beneath the door. The doorknob wiggled a bit and then stopped. A key was inserted into the lock. The knob twisted, and then light poured into the room.

A cacophony of gasps filled the air.

"Ruth? Pepper?" The overhead lights flickered to life.

"Colt!" I shouted, trying to hide my fright. I set the lockbox on the desk and moved past Mom and Piper, as they exchanged looks of dread. "What are you doing here?" I asked, in an abnormally high pitch.

Colt's eyes drifted to the open cash box. "I…saw the lights on from my cabin," he stammered. "Thought I'd better check it out. What are you guys doing here?"

"Oh, well, you know my sister is visiting, and she uh… forgot her toothbrush!" I laughed nervously and glanced over my shoulder. "Yeah, and since the register is closed, we thought we'd just put the money straight into the cash box."

He scrunched his face. "But why were you all hiding in here?"

Mom jumped in to help. "We heard someone enter through the front door and got spooked."

"Yeah, there was a creepy man walking around earlier, and we thought he might have followed us," my sister added. "I'm Piper, by the way." She raised a hand in the air.

Colt lifted his chin to acknowledge her. "Oh. Sorry I scared you."

"No harm done," I said. "Thanks for coming by."

Colt waved, and then turned to leave. The three of us stood in place looking wide-eyed at one another. Once he was out of the building I said, "Whew, that was close."

"Do you think he was really here to check on things?" Mom asked.

"I'm not sure. But we can't go on any longer like this. We need to get to the bottom of this before things get completely out of hand." A thought flashed through my mind. "And I may know just how to do it." I opened a desk drawer and pulled out the campground reservation book. Then we got busy.

# seventeen

By morning light, Piper was deep undercover as "Tricia," the newest resident of Bear Springs Campground. Under the cover of night, we erected my old tent and moved her in to one of the unreserved campsites. She wasn't enthused about having to leave her CPAP behind, but otherwise, Piper was happy for the distraction and ready to unleash a little femme fatale on an unsuspecting male.

The plan was for her to get an eyeball on the spooky new guy, whom we'd codenamed "Squatch." With Piper concealed in her fixed position, and me, Mom, and Harvey doing our normal movements around camp, we figured we'd be able to create a chunky surveillance log on the musty fellow.

I opened the store at 8 a.m., as usual. I was anxious to find out if Piper had pinpointed Squatch's campsite yet, so I gave her a call at my first opportunity.

"Hey, I was just about to text you," she answered. "You guys really need to revamp the lighting in those women's restrooms. I felt like I was trying to put my face on in a black-out this morning."

"Thanks for the suggestion. I'll pass it along," I said, rolling my eyes. "Have you learned anything yet?"

"Yeah. I don't love salsa on my omelets. But ketchup is okay for some reason. Is that weird?"

"Piper, you're at the café? You're supposed to be on post!"

"I'm *supposed* to be blending in with my environment, which is exactly what I'm doing." She lowered her voice. "Actually, I kinda feel like I might have a natural thing for this spy stuff."

I made a face into the phone. "Don't get too carried away." There was a pause, and I had to wait while she asked for a refill on her coffee. "Promise you'll call me the moment you find out where our guy is camped out. I wanna pull his paperwork and see what day he arrived, and if he's there alone or not."

"I'm on it. Tricia out."

"No wait, Piper…Piper? You hung up on me? Ugh!"

Twenty minutes later, my sister breezed into the store with a lipstick-stained to-go cup in her hand. I hated to admit it, but she looked pretty darn good decked out in her Robert Redford *Sundance* ensemble. Those Danner hiking boots probably cost her $400, alone.

No one else was in the shop, so I didn't bother with any pretense. "Piper, what are you doing in here?"

"You can't expect me to just sit at a bare picnic table all day. I need some supplies—it's part of my cover. *I'll pay*," she said, wagging her head at me.

"Fine," I grumbled. "Tell me what you need, so I can get you on your way."

She wandered down the first aisle, carefully considering her options. "I'll know it when I see it," she answered idly. "Ooh." She picked up a nail file. "You wouldn't happen to carry any Essie shades, would you?"

"All our sunglasses are up here at the counter."

She looped her eyes my way. "Oh my gosh, Pepper. That's so embarrassing. No honey, I'm talking about nail polish."

I responded with an ugly face.

Deep lines appeared across her forehead. "Have you *never* had your nails done?"

"Why would I? I bet I could get four rump roasts for the price of one stupid manicure."

Piper shook her head with insult while she returned to the entrance for a shopping basket. She hooked her left arm through the handle, passed her coffee from one hand to the other, and dropped the nail file in. Then she continued her leisure spree, adding three magazines, a seat cushion, and two Fiji waters to her stash.

She was in the personal care section reading the bottle of milk of magnesia when the door opened. My new nemesis, the horrible dad, walked in. We glowered at one another as he passed by. I was desperate to get Piper's attention and let her know we had trouble. But before I could do anything, he parked himself right next to her.

Piper lowered her liquid laxative into the basket and covered it with the July issue of *People*. "Have you seen the children's Tylenol?" he asked.

"It's right here." She pulled a bottle from the shelf and passed it to him. "Is your little one sick?"

"My three-year-old burned himself yesterday. I told him not to go near the fire, but...that kid never listens. It's not too bad. Anyway, that's how kids learn, right?"

Piper grimaced. "I hope he feels better."

"He'll be fine. Hopefully this stuff works so I can get some sleep tonight without all the whining. In fact, maybe I should give him cough syrup instead. Knock him out. You think that'd work better?"

Piper frowned. "I'd just stick with the Tylenol."

"You have kids?"

"Three. But they're grown."

"Really?" He dipped his head in a flirtatious gesture. "I wouldn't have guessed."

I could see the vertical anger crease between her brows. Piper was getting annoyed. "And if I had to guess, I'd say that you got a *late* start on your family." *Atta girl.* "What is it, your second marriage? Third?"

He raised an eyebrow with intrigue. "Second. I'm Ted, by the way." He held out a hand.

"Tricia," she replied. Piper turned and walked away, leaving him hanging. "See ya around."

I could barely keep a straight face as my sister approached the counter. I was starting to see a few similarities in us, after all. And I liked it.

❀ ❀ ❀

It was almost noon—the end of my kitchen shift. Even though it was only a two-hour job, it could be intense. I was definitely looking forward to having Mick back soon. If his rehab continued as planned, we could all go back to our normal jobs in just two weeks. Although part of me had mixed feelings about returning to the old system. I kind of liked being more involved around camp. And what was worse, I wasn't sure what Mom was planning to do once Mick came back. She'd become a part of Bear Springs. I couldn't imagine this place without her now.

I was hanging my apron when Nicole wandered into the back with a load of dirty plates. "Hey kiddo. That banana bread you made this morning sure was a hit."

She placed the dishes in the sink and turned with smile. "You think so? I was just trying to get rid of those rotting things before we had to throw them out."

I laughed. "Did you find that recipe online?"

"Nope. I made it up. When I was younger, I used to love experimenting in the kitchen. You know, before Mom and I moved up here."

"Impressive," I said, nodding my head. "You've got a real gift there."

Her eyes lit up. "Thanks!" She returned to the dining room, just as Harvey and Mom walked into the kitchen to relieve me.

"Hey, you two," I said. "How's everything going? Any Squatch sightings?"

Mom shook her head. "There's been no trace of him yet this morning."

"And thankfully, no new reports of items gone missing," Harvey added. "I know what you girls say you saw last night, but I haven't seen hide nor hair of this Squatch-man. I'm starting to wonder whether he even exists at all," he said, with a wink and a smile.

"You just wait, Harv. We'll make a believer of you," I vowed.

A loud truck pulled to a stop right outside the kitchen door. Mom walked over to see who it was. A car door slammed shut. Mom called though the screen, "Really, Piper? You drove here?"

My sister came waltzing into the kitchen. "That road gets my shoes dusty."

"Pipe-Tricia!" I lowered my voice to a hoarse whisper. "What are you doing? You're blowing your cover! You can't be back here!"

"Ladies." Piper tipped her head at us. "And gentleman," she said, with a slight bow toward Harvey. She flipped her palms outward and continued. "There is no need for alarm. I am pleased to announce that the covert operation has reached its conclusion." Her hands crossed over her heart. "My mission is complete."

My heart was pounding in my chest. "You found Squatch?"

"No," she said, with self-satisfaction. "I found *the thief.*"

"Who is it?" Mom shouted out.

"Here's what happened." Piper shifted her weight around until she'd made herself comfy. "I was in-role at the picnic table, doing what campers do, and BADA-BOOM. I heard voices. But not just any old voices. *Children's* voices…"

Mom stomped her feet and shouted, "Cut the crap, Piper, and tell us who it is!"

"Hold your grannie panties, I'm getting there!" she howled back. She took a moment to collect herself and continued. "There were two boys at the campsite next to mine. I overheard the older boy ordering the younger kid to steal twenty dollars out of his mother's purse and give it to him. Otherwise, he wouldn't be allowed to go to the hot springs with him and all the other kids later. When the younger kid put up a fuss, the older boy told him that several others had already paid to join the club—some buying their way in with things like a cool pair of sunglasses…" Piper paused for comments.

"Nooo…" I breathed. Mom and Harvey looked at one another in shock. "Did you get a look at the kid?" I asked.

"Better than that. I followed him to his campsite."

I raised my hand in the air and smacked my girl with a perfect high-five.

She smiled mischievously. "Oh, there's more." My eyes bulged with greed. "You wanna take a guess as to who the father of this delinquent might be?" she asked.

All the built-up energy I had been enjoying came gushing out, like air from a slashed tire. I closed my eyes, not wanting to face the dreaded truth. "Ted? The horrible dad?" I said, with a cringe. Then I peeked at her with one eye.

She nodded. "And there's still more."

I squeezed both eyes shut again. "What is it?"

"We know him."

"We do?" My eyes shot back open.

"Yeah. I realized who he was when he was flirting with me in the store this morning." Piper looked toward Harvey and Mom. "Does anyone remember the terrible incident that happened here a long time ago, when a boy fell into the river and hit his head on a rock?"

Harvey lifted his hand. "Yes. He nearly drowned. He was pulled unconscious from the water and rushed to the hospital. I remember that day clearly. It was one the worst accidents we ever had here."

"Oh yes, I remember that summer," Mom said. "Was that boy Ted?"

"Oh no," Piper said, with a scornful chuckle. "*Teddy* was the one who pushed the boy into the river."

"Pushed?" Harvey countered. "No, I believe the witnesses said that the boy slipped and fell in."

"Harvey," Piper said. "The witnesses were a bunch of kids. And Ted was their ringleader."

"Oh my gosh," I said, with a shudder of revulsion. "I remember him now."

"Were you girls there when this happened?" Mom's tone was bordering on accusatory.

"Not me," I said, quick to clear my name. "I hated that kid. He was the one who purposely clogged the toilets…and called me *Miss Piggy*."

All eyes turned to Piper. "I was there," she confessed. "We were on the other side of the river, taking turns jumping off the big boulder into the swimming hole. Christopher—that was name of the boy who was injured—he and Teddy were fighting over who got to go next. And then Christopher called him *Beaver*, which was what all the kids called Teddy behind his back."

"As in 'Theodore Cleaver,' from *Leave It to Beaver*," I explained to the others.

Piper nodded. "Right. And Teddy hated that nickname. He got angry and pushed Christopher off the boulder. He fell awkwardly and hit his head on the way into the water." Piper closed her eyes. "It was awful. We thought he was dead. And he would have been, if his younger brother hadn't jumped in after him and pulled him out. My gosh, that little guy couldn't have been more than eight at the time."

"And this Ted just got away with it?" Mom asked. "No one ever told the truth about what happened? He could have killed that boy!"

Piper nodded somberly. "I know. And I still feel terrible about it. When it happened, we were all in shock. Teddy stuck around and did all the explaining when help arrived. He told them that Christopher slipped. And I guess we were all too traumatized—or scared—to speak up." Piper stared at the floor. "I was only nine at the time. And to be honest, that experience has kind of haunted me my whole life. Sadly… Bear Springs was never the same for me after that."

We were all stunned by what we were hearing. I could feel my own righteous anger bubbling up to the surface. I took a deep breath. "I'm not sure what we're waiting for," I said. "I think it's time that Teddy and his children be taught a lesson they'll never forget." I looked around. "Shall we?"

# eighteen

The four of us departed for the campground. We had no plan of attack, just a crude desire for justice.

Ted and his family were gathered at their picnic table for lunch. Curious heads turned our way as we advanced into their territory. Ted's face had already soured, having spotted our posse from a distance. He waited for us to make the first strike.

I stepped out in front. "I told you it wouldn't be good if I had to come back here."

A rebellious laugh shot out. "And what? You had to bring the whole entire family to back you up?"

His wife twisted her body toward us. A look of distress crossed her face. "What is this about?" she pleaded.

"There's nothing to worry about, Amy. These people have just decided they've got nothing better to do than harass our family." He zeroed in on Piper. "I haven't done anything, by the way."

"That's right," I answered. "You haven't. And it's time you did. Time you took responsibility for your actions and taught your kids to do the same." I aimed my focus on his oldest child, a dark-haired boy around twelve years of age. "What's your name?" I asked.

His dad got jumpy and intervened. "Son, you don't have to tell her your name."

I pressed on, undeterred. "Why don't I just go with *Teddy Junior* then." The kid's mouth dropped open so fast, I knew I'd hit the bullseye. Go figure. "Teddy, would you like to tell your mom and dad about the club you've formed? And how you've been forcing children to steal money and other property in order to join?"

"Teddy, don't say anything!" His father turned to us with a contemptuous sneer. "This is outrageous. I'm calling my lawyer." He reached for his phone and said, "Better yet, I'll call Tim Watts—lawyer, personal friend, *and* owner of Bear Springs!"

A booming voice thundered behind me. "Put your phone down, Ted." I whipped my head around. Harvey stepped forward, imposing and strong. "Timothy doesn't own Bear Springs. I do." I glanced over at Piper and Mom. They looked just as shocked as me. "We can settle this right here and now," he continued, "if your son would like to confess to what he's done and return every item that was taken."

"Bull crap. He's not admitting to anything." Ted got to his feet and started clearing the table with a fit. "We are not going to sit here and be judged by you and your...kangaroo court."

"You'll be judged, regardless." Harvey pierced him with his eyes.

"You people are crazy. I have no idea what you are talking about!"

Piper stepped into the spotlight. "Sure you do. BEAVER."

Ted's chin began dripping with sweat. He looked at Piper and laughed nervously. His face contorted. "Who are you?"

"My real name's Piper. I was there when you almost killed Christopher. And I was there when you lied about it. "But now the truth is coming out. And you can either face it like a man, or continue the life of a coward, hiding behind your own lies."

Mom slid in next to Harvey and hooked her arm around his. Her voice was calm, but stern. "Look at your sons, Ted. They're following right in your footsteps. Is that what you want for them?"

"That's it. We're leaving right now. Amy, get the kids packed up. We're leaving this place. And never coming back!"

Harvey latched onto Mom. "That will be just fine."

As soon as we turned to leave, the children began to whine and beg their father to change his mind. Their pleading soon turned to yowling cries—the kind that is meant to punish and manipulate.

I smiled to myself as we marched away. It was going to be a long ride home for that family.

❁ ❁ ❁

Piper and I retrieved her truck from behind the restaurant. With the operation successfully concluded, we drove straight to her campsite to pack up her gear.

"You did a stellar job," I told her, as we folded up tent poles.

She laughed and stuffed her bundle into a nylon bag. "Thanks. You got any more work for me around here?"

"Plenty." I paused and let my smile fade. "How much longer do you plan on keeping this tow truck hostage?"

She turned to me with a frown. "I'm half owner of that vehicle. And the entire business. Taking the truck was simply my way of reminding *him* of that."

The tent lay flat against the ground. I picked up a corner and made a fold. "Are you going to leave…*him*?"

Piper dropped her head and shrugged one shoulder. "I don't know." She groaned with frustration. "I'm dealing with so much anger right now. I don't want to talk to him. I don't want to hear his voice…" I nodded and continued with my work. "One thing's for sure—I need to let my emotions settle down before I make any decisions." A rush of feelings silenced her for several moments. When she spoke again, her voice was squeezed into a whisper. "But I'm scared because, even if I were able to forgive him… What's the point of staying married to someone you don't trust anymore?"

I had a long talk with Stan that evening. Ranger and I took a night stroll, so I could catch Stan up on all the latest happenings without any other ears tuning in. He belly-laughed when I recounted the story about our scary Squatch encounter and how it led to turning my sister into a confidential informant. It felt nice having someone of my own to talk to. It had only been three days since Stan left, which didn't seem possible. So much had happened since he'd been gone. It made me realize how much I missed him and wanted him here.

I was standing under a streetlamp in the empty parking lot outside the store and café when we ended our call. The buildings were closed for the night. The only other lights within view were coming from the cabins on the hill. I could hear the faint sounds of the radio coming from that direction. I smiled, knowing it had to be Nicole, who loved to blast her music in the restaurant whenever we were closed to customers.

I chuckled out loud, recalling a couple weeks back, when she challenged me and Wanda to a '90s dance-off as we were stacking chairs one evening. Being limited to the Robot and a woeful rendition of the Running Man made me no match for Wanda. That skinny girl got her swerve on with some nasty Roger Rabbit and Cabbage Patch moves that made my head spin.

Ranger and I left the parking area and started toward home. Our path narrowed as we merged onto the road that led to the campsites. To our right, the dark forest ascended an endless mountainside. I was replaying the conversation with Stan in my head when a loud snapping noise broke my concentration. My head jerked involuntarily, and Ranger began to growl. We peered into the colorless Ansel Adams wilderness, where everything looked like a black bear. Ranger barked twice before I shushed him. "No bark, Ranger!" I stopped and listened for movement. "Pearl, is that you, honey?" Our deer friend hadn't been around for a while, but I was hoping for a best-case scenario. We stood still for a few more seconds. Whatever it was that had broken that twig was not advancing toward us, and that was all I cared about. "Let's go home, buddy."

❋ ❋ ❋

The next morning, I found myself pacing around the store and checking the parking lot every two minutes for the FedEx guy. Jerry Thompson had promised to get Caroline's envelope in the mail immediately and send it second-day air. So today was the day. And according to the tracking app, Mick's package was supposed to arrive by 10 a.m.

Mick came by at 9:15 and waited with me. He was mostly quiet, and I could certainly understand why. He'd been in a virtual prison for over thirty years, waiting to receive his judgement. Today, at last, his trial would end, and he would know his fate.

A car pulled into the dirt lot. We hustled to the door to see who it was. I wrinkled my nose at Mick—it was just one of our regular campers. The guy left his small sedan running and headed for the ice machine. Just as we turned our backs, we heard a struggle. And then screaming. Mick rushed past me and darted out the door. When I reached the porch, all hell broke loose. A man was carrying Nicole out of the café. Her arms and legs flailed against him wildly, but her small frame was no match for his bulk. Wanda was right behind them, screaming and beating the man's back with her fists, as he stuffed Nicole into the backseat of an old station wagon. He slammed the door shut and knocked Wanda to the ground as he made his way around the car and jumped into the driver's seat. Mick leapt off the porch and sprinted toward the kidnapper's car. He was nearly there when the man spun the tires and sped toward the main exit.

I was momentarily paralyzed, watching Wanda scream Nicole's name, over and over. But then I saw Mick, heading for the running sedan. I called to Wanda as I hurried my way over and dropped into the passenger seat. Mick was already shifting into reverse when Wanda opened the door behind me and hurled herself in. "Go, Mick, go!" she screamed. "He's crazy! He's going to kill her!" Mick peeled out of the parking space and headed for the main road.

Just as he was about to turn left for the exit, I spotted Piper's tow truck, en route to the café. "Mick, stop!" I hollered. "It's Piper! Let me tell her to follow!" I jumped out and waved frantically at my sister as I ran toward her. She rolled her window down with a look of alarm. "Nicole's been abducted! Follow us!" I returned to Mick's car as fast as I could, and we were off.

Wanda was in hysterics as we barreled down the single lane pass. "Please catch him, Mick! We can't let them get away!" Mick didn't answer. His hands were steady on the wheel, and his eyes were clear and focused. He took those mountain curves like they were nothing.

I was on the edge of my seat, hoping each corner would bring the station wagon into view. "Do you know that man, Wanda?" I asked over my shoulder.

She was leaning forward from the middle seat, her head nearly even with ours. Her voice trembled with adrenaline. "It's Ernie Walker, my ex-boyfriend. He's obsessed with Nicole. He got arrested for stalking and vowed to come for her when he got out."

"Is that why you guys came up here? To hide from him?"

"It is. I don't know how he found us, though. We gotta catch them. Please, Mick. He's gonna kill'er!"

Mick gave the gas pedal an extra punch, pressing the tires deeper into the dirt. I tried not to look over the edge, as we hugged the tight curves like a Formula One racecar. We had to be gaining on them.

I turned around to look for Piper, but she was nowhere in sight. There was no way that clunky tow truck could keep pace with us. I just prayed she would stay safe.

Two miles into our chase, we were able to spot their station wagon a few curves ahead.

"I see them! We're closing in, Mick. Just hold what you got, buddy." I glanced over at him. His eyes were burning with an intensity I'd never seen in a human being. His jaw tightened as he delicately added more pressure to the pedal. Our car began to fishtail around every corner.

"I think you need to let off the gas just a bit, Mick. We're losing traction." He didn't respond. Mick was in a zone, somewhere very far away. We raced around the next corner. "You need to slow down a little…Mick, STOP!" He slammed on the brakes, causing us to skid dangerously close to the edge. We came to an abrupt halt, just behind a wreck. Ahead of us, the station wagon was nose-to-nose with a FedEx truck. White steam rose between the two.

The station wagon's rear lights lit up. Ernie was trying to back out. Before he could create any space for himself, Mick squeezed right beside him at an angle, pinning the station wagon against the side of the mountain. Ernie was locked in tight on three sides, and unable to open any doors.

Wanda began to scream. "Nicole! Get out of the car! Nicole!" She and her daughter were nearly face-to-face, separated only by two sets of windows. Wanda banged on the glass.

Mick was also trapped in his seat. "Pepper, get out!" he ordered. I opened my door and exited the car. Mick scooted himself across the front seats and jumped out. He ran to the rear of the station wagon and tried to open the hatchback, but Ernie had everything locked.

Nicole was pushed up against the rear passenger window, as far from Ernie as she could get. He was now twisting in his seat, trying to reach back to grab her.

Mick returned to the sedan. "Wanda, I need in there!" Wanda scampered out of the backseat and joined me on the road, while Mick hurried to take her spot. We watched helplessly as he rolled down her window, and then quickly positioned himself across the seat on his back. Nicole leaned back just in time to avoid Mick's foot, which came bursting through her window.

Ernie was in a struggle against his own girth, trying to get himself twisted around in his seat so he could try to gain some control over his abductee. Knowing his prize was about to get away from him, he grunted like a wild animal and bucked with all his might, attempting to break through his seat. It was in that moment of savagery that I realized I was looking at Squatch.

Wanda and I jumped up and down like cheerleaders on the sidelines. "Go, Nicole! Get out!" Squatch's chair was rocking with such force, I knew it wouldn't be long before something gave. Mick crawled to his knees and leaned out his window. Nicole ducked her head through the shattered glass and reached an arm out. Mick took hold of her right hand and yelled, "Give me your other hand. I'll pull you through!"

She thrust her left arm out, and then pulled it back suddenly. "He's got my foot!" she yelled. Squatch had figured out to recline his seat and now had a firm grip of Nicole's ankle.

A game of tug of war began. "I've got you, Nicole," Mick breathed. "I won't let him take you. I promise."

Nicole screamed in pain. "He's hurting me! Ow, let go of me!" Squatch had her right foot pinned under his arm.

"Give me your other hand," urged Mick.

"I can't!" she screamed.

"You've got to. It'll free up your other leg to kick. Please, trust me!" Nicole cast her left arm out toward Mick, like she was throwing a lifesaver. Mick caught her hand and braced himself against the door. Nicole was suspended in a Super-man pose, supported only by her belly, which lay across the glass-covered window frame. "Now kick, Nicole! Kick!"

Wanda and I joined in with our invisible pom poms. "Kick him, Nicole! Smash his face in!" Her feet began to flut-ter, like she was motoring herself down the swimming lane with a kickboard. "Harder, harder!" I yelled. Her free foot landed a pointed toe box right into Squatch's eye socket. He yelped and reached for his face, yielding the grip on her leg. With the sudden loss of suspension, Mick fell backward and dragged Nicole through both windows, until she beached herself right on top of him. Wanda screamed and climbed in after her.

A loud screech pulled my attention from the scene. Piper put her tow truck in park and hopped to the ground. "Pep-per!" She ran to me, her eyes wide with fear. "Are you hurt?"

I put a calming hand on her arm. "We're fine. We didn't have the accident. They did." I pointed toward the station wagon and the FedEx truck. Although the truck didn't appear to have any damage, the airbag had deployed and knocked the driver out cold.

"I thought you said Nicole had been kidnapped?" she said, still trying to understand.

"I did. Squatch dragged her out of the café and tried to do a runner. Mick just now got her back."

"What? Squatch?" Piper put her hands on her head and spun around to view the chaotic scene.

Mick appeared next to me, breathing heavily. "Hey. This ain't over yet, ladies. I'm turning this car around, and then you all are taking Nicole and heading back to Bear Springs. Piper, can I borrow your tow truck?"

"Keys are in the ignition," she said.

"What are you going to do?" I asked warily.

Mick's voice become gravelly. "I'm gonna make things right."

Nicole and Wanda remained in the back seat, clinging to one another. Mick put the sedan into reverse and steered past the tow truck, until he found a spot wide enough to carefully turn it around. We trotted after him on foot. He slipped the car into park and hopped out. "Now please. All of you, go!"

Piper moved toward the front passenger door and turned to take one more look at Squatch. He was still trapped in the driver's seat, but with our vehicle no longer keeping him in place, nothing was stopping him from trying to get away in his car. She pointed and screamed, "He's on the move!"

I turned around. Sure enough, Squatch was backing his car up, positioning himself to try and squeeze past the FedEx truck. "He'll never make it through there. It's too narrow!" I exclaimed. Mick sprinted to the tow truck and climbed in.

"Yeah, but if he does make it, he's gone," Piper said, with her hands to her mouth. "My truck is way too wide to follow."

The station wagon approached the FedEx truck and began to crawl past slowly. Its tires were just inches from the cliff.

"Hurry, Mick! You've got to stop him before he gets through," I hollered. Mick put the truck into first gear and lurched forward. He quickly shifted to second and gassed it, trying to close the distance before it was too late. The station wagon continued its slow roll toward freedom, as the tires sent loose dirt clods on a mile-long freefall.

Squatch was two feet from making his escape, when Mick was forced to let off the gas and stomp the brakes hard. The tow truck came gliding in behind the station wagon like a perfectly thrown curling stone. Whether any bumpers actually touched, we'll never know—Piper's brakes screamed loud enough to cover up a bombing. What I did witness, however, was the Squatch-mobile beginning to slide sideways, just before it went hiney-first over the side of the mountain. And when it finally came to a rest, barely a *poof* was made.

# nineteen

My first phone call was to Stan. After I explained everything that happened, he got the authorities on their way. They came, quickly took our statements, and released us. No one was going to miss Ernie Walker.

As for the FedEx guy, he woke up from his airbag nap just in time for me to sign for Mick's package before we left.

Piper and the ladies pulled out in the sedan, headed back to camp. Mick climbed into the driver's seat of the tow truck. "You all right to drive?" I asked. He'd been awfully quiet since the incident.

"I'm fine," he answered, in a raspy voice. "Just got a lot goin' on in my head."

I walked around to the passenger side and threw the large envelope on the seat before hoisting myself up. "I'd be glad to drive, if you wanna read…"

He looked anxiously at the packet. "I'd be tempted to if it weren't for this curvy road. I already feel a little queasy as it is." I gave him a tired smile and clicked on my seat belt. He must have been dying to know what was in there.

We drove the rest of the way in silence. When the terrain finally opened up and the "Welcome to Bear Springs" sign came into view, Mick jerked the truck off the road and stopped in a patch of tall grass and wildflowers.

The sudden move startled me. "You okay?"

His shoulders stiffened. "I have to know what's in there, Pepper. I can't wait any longer." He looked at me with those pleading, sad eyes. "But the truth is, I'm scared to death. Would you mind reading it to me?"

I could feel Mick's agony in my own chest, like a parent who suffers their child's pain. "Of course." I mustered one last smile of encouragement, and then ripped the tab across the face of the mailer. Reaching through the opening, I pulled out two separate envelopes. I set the bulkier of the two down and opened the first. It was a handwritten letter. I took a deep breath and read aloud.

> *Hello Mick,*
>
> *I found you at last. There are so many things I wish to tell you—but I'd like to begin with an apology. I'm sure you have wondered what happened to me. You probably feared the worst. And for putting you through that for these many years, I am truly, deeply sorry.*
>
> *With regards to the incident in Tijuana, I want you to know that I was never physically harmed. What took place was essentially a botched kidnapping. I was rescued by the Mexican police after being held for three days by a street gang. I returned safely to the States, completely unscathed.*
>
> *I have often wondered what happened to you and the others that night. There was a strong smell of*

*blood in the van. I pray none of you were injured too badly in the fight.*

*I need you to know that I never assigned any blame to you or the others for what happened. You were outnumbered and taken by surprise. You fought valiantly and did everything you possibly could to save me. I am forever grateful for the danger you all placed yourselves in for my sake.*

*Many of the memories from that incident are starting to fade, thankfully. But one remains as powerful as ever—the last image I saw before my captors blindfolded me. It was you, Mick, sprinting after the van with the most searing look in your eyes. I'm still brought to tears every time I think of it.*

*I wish I could explain why I didn't contact you immediately after my release. To this day, I can only offer a host of lame excuses for myself. I was young, I was in shock. I was also scared and unsure what had happened to you. Furthermore, I didn't want to get you in trouble with your commanding officers, which is why I never reported the incident. But there was another factor, which I came to learn about just a few days later. And it sidetracked me for a good while. I found out that I was pregnant. With our child.*

*And now (deep breath), I've arrived at the most difficult part of the letter—attempting to explain how I could have kept your daughter from you. I'm sure you have a range of emotions running through you at this moment, and you are entitled to every one of those feelings. Please know that it was never my intention to keep her from you. I hope you can forgive me. So much happened all at once. I moved in with my aunt, went back to school, had the pregnancy to deal with…and then I became a new mommy. It was a couple years before I finally came up for air and realized I needed to let you know you were a dad. I contacted the Marine Corp, hoping to get an address for you, so I could send you a letter. But by that time, you had left. I tried many times over the years to find you, Mick. It seemed you'd fallen off the face of the earth. But…since you're reading this now, we've obviously managed to reconnect somehow. And that gives me great peace.*

*There's just one last thing I need to do, before I go. And that is to introduce you to your daughter, Fey. I could write volumes about our girl. She is bright and witty and caring. And she has a lot of you in her. I always noticed that. She inherited your inquisitive mind, that's for sure. Growing up, she was always begging me to tell her stories about her daddy. I tried to remember all the tales you ever shared about your childhood. Her favorite was the one about you and your brother, when you guys jumped onto a moving freight train, and your parents had to drive two hundred miles to bring you home! How is Darrel, anyhow? And your folks? Are they well? Please send them my regards.*

*Fey is married now, with two kids and counting. She still asks about you. With a family of her own, she is all the more curious about her roots, and she strongly desires for her children to be raised around loved ones. She asked me to include her telephone number with my letter. It would mean the world to her to hear from you.*

*I can't tell you how good it feels to be talking to you now. I could go on forever. But I will end it here. Thank you, Mick, for being in my life. Thank you for giving me an incredible daughter and leading me to a wonderful, happy life. I am forever grateful to you. I pray this letter finds you well.*

*Love always,*
*Lina*

I folded the letter and passed it to Mick. With shaky hands he gently reopened it and shuffled to the last page. His eyes were filled with tears as he quietly meditated on her final words.

I reached for the other envelope and slipped out the contents. Lina had sent him an assortment of photos and mementos, capturing the major milestones in Fey's life. She included everything from baby pictures, to report cards and team photos, all the way up to Fey's wedding pictures. There were even photos of the grandbabies. One boy and one girl. I placed everything back in the envelope and held it out to him.

Mick nodded his head and collected everything together. Then he opened his door. "I think I'm just gonna sit out here a while," he said. "I'll make my way back."

"You got it." I hopped out and took his place in the driver's seat. Through the rear-view mirror, I watched as he found a spot in the dirt and sat with his back against a chunk of granite. I took one last look as I pulled away. Mick laid the package in his lap. Then he leaned his head back and raised his open hands to the sky.

❋ ❋ ❋

Stan called that night to see how everything had turned out. And also, to pass along some incredible information. Trevor's autopsy results had come in earlier that week, and Stan had been working on his closing report the past few evenings from his hotel room. He didn't want to tell me about it until his document was officially approved and in the system.

The findings were not what anyone was expecting. The medical examiner had filed the manner of death as an accident. The cause of death was drowning, with a snake bite as the influencing factor.

Stan pooled all the information to cite the most probable sequence of events, leading to Trevor's death. It was now believed that after parking his car at Harris Lake, Trevor entered the woods, possibly to meet someone, or to find a discreet location to relieve himself. There he encountered a rattlesnake, which struck his calf. After being bit, he walked an unknown distance to the lake. He waded in, presumably to wash the wound. While there, the venom took effect. Trevor's body went into a state of shock, leading to a loss of consciousness. Water samples taken from his lungs proved not only that he was alive when he collapsed in the water, but also, that it was indeed Harris Lake and not Juniper Lake, where he died.

There were other surprising discoveries, as well. On the outside of Trevor's clothing, the medical examiner found traces of an unusual type of algae. He also encountered the remnants of an even more distinctive type of salamander. Both rare species shared one common link—they could only be found in dark caves.

Stan was beside himself when he shared those final details with me. Trevor's autopsy results had accomplished the impossible. Not only did they validate Stan's wild hypothesis about how the young man's body had traveled from one lake to the other, but on a larger scale, they provided the means to turn legend into history. Stan's official government report would forever stand as the cornerstone for all future and past cases, where a subterranean river could be given as the most reasonable explanation for a mystery like Trevor's.

❀ ❀ ❀

One of my old bosses loved to tell me how she always got horribly sick at the end of each semester in college. It was like clockwork, she said. As soon as she put her pencil down after her last final, she could feel it coming on.

The body is amazing that way. Whether it's pushing someone through exams or clinging to life until it feels the grasp of a familiar hand, it will go as far as it's needed, and then it will take its rest.

It had been seven days since Nicole's abduction, and I still felt like a zombie. If there were ever a time when I was going to contract shingles, it was now. Who would've thought someone could breeze through thirty years as a dispatcher, only to get PTSD after two months as a camp host? It was embarrassing. I hadn't been this disgusted with myself since I puked up a whole bag of fried wonton strips. At least I finally figured out why grocery stores don't sell those things in the snack aisle...

I'd spent all week trying to work through the recent events in my mind. Piper was a big help. She hung out with me every day and let me go on about all the drama that had taken place since I'd moved up there. I told her Trevor's story from beginning to end and gave her all the gory details about

Mick flatlining on the kitchen floor. We gossiped about Daddy and Harvey, and what kind of secret they might have been sheltering. I even shared some stuff about me and Stan.

As it turned out, my sister was a pretty good listener. And kind, too. Piper told me she was worried about me and had never seen me down in the dumps like this. She said since Daddy died, she'd always counted on me to be the strong one, to make everything right and to hold us all together. "Don't go all soft on me now," she said.

I had been attributing my malaise to undigested events. But after talking through it all, I realized it wasn't the past that was bothering me. It was the future. At some point Mom would be going home, and Piper, too. And now with Ernie Walker dead, Nicole and Wanda had no reason to stay. Then there was Harvey, who was slowing down physically and facing pressure to sell. I finally realized what was really eating at me. Bear Springs was in jeopardy. And with it, my entire future.

# <u>twenty</u>

When I woke up on Saturday morning, my room was bathed in red. I looked out the window and saw the most beautiful colors scattered across the sky. But I knew what it meant. And it wasn't good. We were now in the second half of summer, which began the wildfire season. I'd heard a few reports of fires earlier in the week and had even smelled a little smoke when the wind was right. Judging by the looks of this blazing sunrise, the flames were spreading.

Ranger and I stopped by the café for a quick bite to eat. Harvey was there, along with Wanda and Nicole.

"Hey, guys," I said. "What's the word on these wildfires? They look like they're getting worse."

Harvey sipped his coffee and made a grave face. "It's not looking good. The winds changed yesterday afternoon, and the fires have been advancing in our direction all night long."

I felt a chill go down my spine. "Will someone tell us if we need to evacuate?"

"Yes," he said, with a nod. "And I've already checked in with the Forest Service this morning. They've assured me they'll give us plenty of notice, should the need for an evacuation arise. But for now, we're on standby."

"I should call Stan. He and Cinnamon are supposed to be driving back today. I hope they don't get delayed."

"I wouldn't be surprised if they did. There are plenty of road closures out there." Harvey walked toward the exit. "Let me know if he's got any updates on the fire. I'm heading down to speak with your mother, to let her know I'll be managing things from up here today." He pushed the door open and stepped outside.

I entered the kitchen, where Wanda was mixing a large bowl of pancake batter. She must have noted the worried look on my face. "It ain't no big deal. We get put on standby every summer," she said.

"It seems like we ought to be doing something, though. There must be some kind of protocol. Should we be making announcements, or closing off the trails or something? What if someone's on a hike when the Forest Service orders us out?"

She moved the batter aside and began cracking eggs into a separate container. "Harvey's got a checklist with all that kinda stuff on it. I'm sure he's already taking care of it. Hey, could you grab me another carton of eggs?"

A frown settled on my face as I crossed the kitchen. "If it were up to me and we were on standby for an evacuation, I think I might close the restaurant and the store and have all hands on deck. Wouldn't you?"

"I dunno. Harvey says he don't want anybody to panic."

I tilted my head and silently wondered how many people died needlessly each year, because someone in charge didn't want to cause a panic.

"Maybe I'll go find Harv and look at this checklist of his. Come on, Ranger." I exited through the back door, surprised to see how quickly the sky had darkened. The smoke had found its way to our basin in the sky and was settling right in.

We passed by the back of the store. Through the rear window I spotted Harvey, seated at his desk in the office. I picked up the pace. As Ranger and I cornered the building, my cell phone rang. I stopped in front of the general store to take the call.

"Stan! Please tell me you're on your way?"

"We are, but the roads are a mess with all these wildfires. We're gonna have to go around them. Gonna add a couple hours to our trip, I'm afraid."

"Aw..."

"And that's assuming we can get there at all. I got off the phone with my boss a minute ago, and he said they just gave evac orders to Twin Pines."

"Oh geez."

"Yeah. That is not far from you guys."

I felt my stomach drop. "I should probably go, so I can give Harvey the update."

"Okay. And listen. I know Harvey's been through this drill a time or two, but…this one's a little too close for comfort, Pepper. And the way that fire's burning right now—it's picking up steam and heading straight for Bear Springs. Promise me you'll be careful, please."

My throat ached as a small lump began to form. "I will."

Ranger and I trotted up the steps and entered the store. I locked the door behind us. "Harv, you back there?" I called, as I made my way toward the office.

"Yes, Pepper."

I hustled down the center aisle and parked myself in the doorway. "Just got off the phone with Stan," I said, slightly out of breath. "Twin Pines is being evacuated." Harvey's eyes went blank. "I think that makes us next on the list." He swiveled toward his desk and picked up a piece of paper. "I was thinking we might want to shut down all normal operations and try to get ahead of this thing."

"Right," he said, with a reluctant sigh. Then he nodded. "Best to err on the side of caution."

I was shaking with nervous energy. "What should I do first?"

"Notify all staff members to stop what they're doing and report here to me, please."

"What about the people at the campground?"

"I'll take the bullhorn down and make an announcement as soon as I hand out a few assignments."

I ran next door to tell the ladies to close the café and see Harvey for instructions. I also tasked Nicole with texting a notification to Colt. On the way to Mick's cabin, I rang Piper and told her and Mom to get up to the store as soon as possible.

Mick and I jogged back to the store together. Harvey had already sent Nicole and Wanda out to post signs and block trails with traffic cones. When we got there, he gave Mick a set of instructions on how to properly close the kitchen. I was tasked with creating a register of all our guests, so we could account for each party as they evacuated. In just a few minutes, that tiny office space had transformed into a legitimate operations center.

By the time I finished my list, everyone was away completing their assignments. I decided to step outside to check the conditions and give Stan another call. Ranger followed me as I descended the porch steps and walked toward the road to get a full view of the sky. I turned in a circle to take it all in. There was an eerie orange glow to the world, as though the ether itself were aflame. I took a deep breath and felt pain at the back of my lungs. The air quality had diminished rapidly.

I put a call through to Stan. He answered right away. "Pepper? What's happening out there?"

"We haven't had any official word yet, but we're making preparations to leave."

"Good. Because I've been sitting here thinking about what a nightmare it would be, trying to get all those cars through the pass…" He sighed. "And if the fire somehow jumped around you and blocked your only way out—you'd be trapped with absolutely nowhere to go."

"I know, Stan. This is definitely not a great place to be caught in a fire. But…let's try not to think that way. The winds could change, and it could all be fine."

He moaned. "I just wish I could be there with you. So I knew you were okay."

My eyes welled up with tears. "Why don't you step on it then, and get yourself here?"

His voice trembled with emotion. "I'm doin' my best, darlin'. Believe me."

After we hung up, I went back to the store to make an extra copy of the list I'd put together. I was reading over my work when I stepped into the office and bumped right into someone.

"Oh! I didn't think anybody was back here." I put my hand over my heart and took a step back, into the doorway. "Tim?" Even though he was only an arm's length away, I had to squint to recognize him. His eyes were hidden by sunglasses. "What are you doing here? You know we're about to be evacuated, right?" I stared at my distorted face in his mirrored lenses, waiting for a response. After an uncomfortable length of silence, I noticed a folded piece of paper in his right hand. He must have seen me looking, because he opened his sport coat and tried to slip it into the interior pocket. "What do you have?" I reached out and ripped the sheet from his hands. I glanced down. It was the latest bank statement, which had just come in the mail. "What is this, Tim?" I unfolded it and started scanning the transactions, turning my back to him in the process.

Tim darted around and wrestled the paper out of my hands. "Mind your business, Pepper." Then he pushed me back a step before turning and striding toward the front exit. I quickly regained my balance, although my brain remained in shock over the ruthless altercation. Before he could reach the door, I heard a jingle, followed by Harvey's voice.

"Timothy! What are you doing here? Don't tell me you've come to help…"

"Harvey!" I yelled from the back of the store. "Don't let him go," I screamed, skittering up the aisle.

Harvey's face filled with alarm. His head pivoted back and forth between me and his son. "What's the meaning of this?"

"I'm here on urgent business, Dad. It can't wait."

"Harvey, don't listen to him! I caught him in your office, stealing bank records!"

Keeping his eyes on his father, Tim stretched his palm out to shush me. "Can we go somewhere to talk, please?"

"It was him!" I shouted.

Harvey raised his hands in confusion. "Everyone, please. Let's just calm down for a moment. Pepper, can you please explain to me what exactly is going on here?"

I jumped right in. "Remember when you had concerns about missing funds? Tim was the one who took the money! On the day of Trevor's memorial, he accessed the Bear Springs account from your computer and transferred five thousand dollars to himself. And he snuck in here today to get rid of the physical evidence. He hoped you'd never notice!"

Harvey's eyes narrowed. "Take off those glasses, Timothy."

Tim lowered his head and slowly pulled the shades from his face. Both eyes were nearly swollen shut. Before Harvey or I could respond, Tim shook his head and said, "It's fine, Dad. Everything is under control. In fact, I'm here with amazing news. I have a buyer who's offering ten million for Bear Springs. The guy is literally waiting by the phone. All we need is the green light from you, and we can get the paperwork started today…"

A loud ring tone filled the air. Harvey put his phone to his ear and received the dreaded news. It was time to leave. He hung up and turned to place his hand on the door. Looking over his shoulder, he said, "Go home, Timothy." He pushed the door open and descended the steps, toward his golf cart. Tim ran after him.

"Wait a second, Dad. Let me stay and help. What do we need to do? Are there insurance papers somewhere? What about the deed? I can grab those."

Harvey sat in his cart and looked up at Tim. "If you really want to help, get in your car and drive to the end of the pass. Make sure no one comes through. We can't have anything blocking our way out of here."

Tim put his sunglasses back on. He trotted to his black Porsche Boxster and sped away.

I lifted both eyebrows and took a deep breath. "What now, boss?"

Harvey pointed in the direction of the campground. A loaded vehicle was headed our way. "Looks like the exodus has already begun," he said. "We need to check everyone off the list as they leave. I'll get these people's names while you run in and grab your paper and clipboard. And then I need to get down to the campsites to get everyone moving. The sooner our guests get out of here, the sooner we get out of here."

The next two hours felt like an eternity as I stood alongside the road, stopping every family before they left. I was growing more uneasy with each car that passed through my checkpoint. Although I couldn't see any flames, I knew the fire was close. The air had grown heavier and harder to breathe. And Ranger's coat was now covered in a light-grey film.

When only two families remained, Nicole relieved me so I could run to the camper and pack my car. Mom and Piper had already loaded their things into the tow truck and moved to the store parking lot, where we were instructed to stage our vehicles. I hurried home with Ranger and spent twenty minutes hauling my "go items" to the Corolla. Then I locked the camper, and prayed it wasn't for the last time.

I took the long way to the staging area, making sure the campsites were clear. When I arrived in the parking lot, the rest of the group had finished their jobs and were now moving boxes of files from the office. They stashed them in any car that still had some extra space.

After the last load, Harvey gathered us in. "We've got four cars for eight people. I want two bodies in every car—I don't care who rides with whom. But we all stick together, you hear? I'll be the lead vehicle. I want Piper behind me, then Pepper, and Colt, you'll be driving the tail car. Now visibility is going to be bad, so we're going to take it very slow through the pass. Once we get down the mountain, we have rooms reserved at the Red Lion Inn. Are there any questions?" He scanned the group. "No? All right then. Let's get moving, gang."

The group split into teams quickly. Harvey and Mick pulled onto the road first and waited. Piper slid in behind their truck, with Mom as her passenger. I pulled up next, with Wanda and Ranger in my car. Bringing up the rear were Colt and Nicole in the Bear Springs truck.

We moved out like a convoy creeping through enemy land. Thick with smoke, even the air suggested we were in a combat zone. I could feel my teeth clenching the way they did when I was a child, as we edged our way through the fifteen-mile-long chokepoint. Wanda was tense as well, although her shoulders seemed to relax a bit once we'd passed the scene of last week's accident. Our small troop had been through one war after another this summer. If we could just get through this last battle, I thought, maybe we would find rest ahead.

After spending an hour carving our way around the mountainside, we hit the paved road and turned downhill. With each passing minute, the air seemed a bit clearer. We continued our caravan toward Fresno.

I called Stan to let him know we'd made it out safely and were headed for the hotel. I invited him to meet us there, but he'd just received orders to report directly to work to help deal with the fires. I couldn't believe it. We were leaving the danger area, and he was heading into it. Hot tears rolled down my cheeks.

# twenty-one

It was lunchtime when we checked into the hotel. Mom, Piper, and I decided to share a room. After living in my camper together the last several weeks, it seemed the natural thing to do. Heck, I'd even grown accustomed Piper's nighttime ruckus. In fact, I'd offered to share a bed with my sister, but Mom said she preferred sleeping beside someone who *looked* like a swamp creature, rather than a dog who *smelled* like one. Fair enough.

Before the group split up, Harvey had invited everyone to either order room service or to eat lunch in the hotel restaurant, so we could put our meals on his tab. The Rose ladies were so starved, we wasted no time picking up the phone and placing an order.

When the food arrived, Mom grabbed her tray and headed for the door. "I'm going to check on Harvey," she said. "Make sure he got himself a bite to eat."

Piper and I turned on the television and spread out between the two beds. With a nose for French fries, Ranger snuggled right up next to me. Before we could take our first bites, however, Mom came bursting back into the room.

"Girls! Harvey and Tim are having a big argument! Come quickly!"

I threw my meal aside and scooted to the edge of the bed as fast as I could. "What's Tim doing here?"

"He must have followed us. Please, it sounds really bad!"

Piper and I trotted down the hallway with Mom. Sure enough, the heated exchange could be heard several doors down.

Tim was in a rage. "I am out of time!" he bellowed. "If I don't have a deal by tonight, I'm as good as dead!"

We reached Harvey's door and banged with our fists. "Harvey, open the door!"

Tim's voice boomed back. "Don't you move, old man! You're going to sit there and you're going to talk to me. You at least owe me that!"

"I don't owe anything, son."

Mom shouted, "I'm calling security!"

"No, Ruth," Harvey answered from somewhere behind the door. "It's all right. Timothy isn't going to do anything he'll regret." The room fell silent. A few seconds later, the door opened, and we all flooded in.

Mom went straight for Tim, whose face looked a lot like mine the morning after a big soy sauce overdose. "Timothy, I want you to leave this instant."

Tim snapped right back. "Who do you think you are?" He leered at her with his slitted eyes. Then he swiveled his head toward me and Piper. "This is a Watts family matter. You Roses need to mind your own business."

Mom stuck her chest out and replied, "Oh really? Well, let me tell you something, Timothy…"

Harvey quickly stepped between the two and extended his arms. "That's enough! Please, everyone. Let's just calm down." He turned toward Mom with apologetic eyes. Then he sighed and lowered his arms. "I think it's time we all had a talk. Let's see if we can find a place where we can sit, shall we?"

We managed to hold our hostilities in as we rode the elevator to the main level, where Harvey located an empty meeting hall. The room was staged for a speaking event, with two sections of chairs and a walkway down the middle. Harvey led us to the head of the room and asked us to take a seat. He stood before us with his hands in his pockets and a look of distress on his face.

"I hope you all will forgive me," he began. "I wasn't prepared for this." His eyes flickered toward Mom. "Not that I haven't given much thought to it. On the contrary, I have wanted this for years." He took a deep breath. "It was only out of respect for Jack that I never said anything before." Piper's elbow dug into my side.

"When I was eighteen, my mother confided in me. Risking her own reputation, her marriage, even her relationship with her only child…she came forward with a very hard truth." Harvey's voice broke with emotion. "And the truth was that George Watts was not my biological father." He blinked tears from his eyes. "Henry Rose was."

"What?" Piper blurted out. "Henry Rose? My grandfather?"

Harvey lowered his misty eyes and nodded. "Your father and I were half-brothers."

Tim laughed with disbelief. "You're telling me that you aren't actually a Watts?"

"And neither are you," Harvey replied candidly. "Every person in this room is a Rose."

"You're my uncle?" I said, through trembling lips.

Piper turned toward Tim with disgust. "You're my cousin?"

Tim jumped out of his seat. "This is the most ludicrous garbage I've ever heard in my life!"

Harvey reached out. "Timothy, please sit down."

"Dad didn't want to expose his own father's infidelity," I said, wiping a tear with my sleeve. "That's what you two fought about in Mexico."

Harvey nodded. "He didn't want any relationships destroyed over a brief summer romance that had ended two decades earlier. To him, nothing good could come of releasing that information. And the more I thought about it, the more satisfaction I took, just knowing that Jack and I were finally able to understand the special bond we always shared." There was a long stretch of silence, while the four of us sat speechless.

"So…" Harvey clapped his hands together. "This brings me to point number two."

Piper shook her head in disbelief. "He's got another bomb, everyone…"

Harvey gave a fleeting smile and then locked eyes with mine. "Pepper," he said. I felt my heart jump in my chest. "It's been nearly a year since you rang me out of the blue and asked to join us at Bear Springs." My hands started to sweat. "And the moment I heard your voice on that telephone, my heart leapt with joy because…I finally knew who my successor would be." I swallowed hard and felt the tears begin to swell. "There's no one better suited for the job. And there's no better time than the present." Harvey held out his hands.

"Pepper Rose, would you do me the honor of being the next owner-manager of Bear Springs Campground?"

With tears pouring down my face, I left my seat and took Harvey's hands. "It would be a dream come true." He released my hands and folded me up in a massive hug. I closed my eyes and cried softly into his shirt. And for one precious moment, I was embracing my father again.

"No!" Tim flew to his feet, knocking his chair to the ground. "You can't do this. Bear Springs belongs to the Watts family!"

Harvey took a protective step in front of me, and shook an angry finger at Tim. "Don't you pretend to care about Bear Springs, Timothy. We all know what you'd do with it if you had your druthers."

Tim's face burned hot. He threw one last nasty glare at the group and then bolted up the aisle. He hit the crash bar with a *bang*. As the door flung open, he turned and said, "I hope your precious Bear Springs burns to the ground. Then we'll all have nothing."

❀ ❀ ❀

Sleep did not come easy that night. My brain was like a faulty television set, switching from channel to channel all night long. There was so much to think about, starting with the enormous responsibility of taking over the campground. Lying in the dark, I started a mental list of short and long-term goals that I hoped to accomplish—assuming Bear Springs survived the fire.

That, of course, was an entirely different subject to agonize over. Stan had given me a final fire update around ten o'clock that night. He said the fire was still advancing, but because slope winds change direction from day to night, we wouldn't know until morning which path it would take as it burned across our part of the mountain.

The thought of losing Bear Springs was unimaginable. But the more I contemplated the situation, the more I found myself worrying about Stan, and not Bear Springs. I hated that he had to be there, right in the middle of the danger. My anguished thoughts turned to fervent prayers, as I visualized chunks of burning fuel rolling downhill and starting spot fires all around. *Please, don't let anything happen to him. I love him.*

At 6:12 the next morning, I was awoken by a gentle knock on the door. Ranger and I scrambled out of bed to investigate. I lowered my eye to the peep hole and let out a noise I never knew I could make.

I ripped the door open and jumped into Stan's arms. The door slammed behind me as we spilled into the hallway. Ranger tore up and down the carpeted corridor, equally excited to see Cinnamon.

"You smell like smoke," I said, still squeezing him tight.

He chuckled. "Sorry about that."

"No, I don't care. I'm just so happy you're okay. I can't believe you're here!"

We separated and looked longingly at one another. "I came as soon as I could," he said. "So I could give you the news in person."

I searched his eyes. "Is it good?"

A smile broke across his face. "Bear Springs is safe. The fire went around the east side."

I squealed and jumped up and down. "That is wonderful!" I heaved an enormous sigh of relief.

Stan took my hands in his. "Yes. You all can go home now." His smile slowly waned as a look of concern began to pull at his eyes.

"What is it, Stan? Something's wrong, isn't it?"

He shrugged. "Everything's okay. It's just…my house didn't make it."

"Oh no! It burned down? Were you able to save anything?"

He shook his head. "I couldn't get anywhere near it. Everything's gone."

I pressed my hands to my lips. "This is terrible. I'm so sorry."

He smiled sadly and said, "But it does make you realize what's important in your life." He gazed deep into my eyes. "And I still have that."

A door opened down the hall. Harvey stepped out in a bath robe and slippers. "Stanley!" He shuffled his stiff legs toward us. Do we have any news?"

"Bear Springs is clear," he replied. "You made it, Mr. Watts."

Harvey smacked his palms together and let out a *whoop*. As our noisy jubilation continued, more doors began to open. It wasn't long before the entire crew was gathered in the hallway, celebrating the news.

In the midst of the chatter, Harvey raised his hands in the air. "Hey, gang? How about we celebrate over some breakfast? Let's meet next door at the Waffle House in thirty minutes."

❀ ❀ ❀

We were given our own wing, a semi-private area reserved for large parties. As we passed jelly packets and syrup dispensers around, word spread about the fate of Stan's house. Harvey didn't waste a second inviting Stan to share the Watts cabin with him, for as long as he needed. And Stan gratefully accepted.

Harvey also used the opportunity to announce my promotion. Everyone was warm and supportive. But none more so than Colt, who surprised me by leaving his seat to personally congratulate me and tell me that he knew Bear Springs "was in great hands" under my care, and that he looked forward to having me as his boss.

Before we finished our meal, I stood and made my first speech. It wasn't long, and I didn't cry. I just wanted everyone in that room to know how much they meant to me.

When breakfast was over, we pushed through the glass doors and turned up the walkway toward the hotel. It was time to check out and get back home. Outside, the air smelled clean and fresh. The sun was still caught behind the tall mountain, but the wind had blown the smoke out of view. The heavens were blue again.

As we walked past the restaurant windows, I caught a glimpse of Mick, coming up behind me. He grabbed my arm and gave it a light tug. "Can I have a word with you? And Harvey, too?"

"Sure," I said, with a look of surprise. I stepped to the side. "Harv, do you have a second?" He turned around and walked back toward us, while the rest of the group continued ahead.

The three of us huddled together in front of the Waffle House. Mick dropped his head and kicked a pebble into the parking lot. He was making me nervous.

"Everything okay?" I asked.

He looked up with glassy eyes. "I wanted to let you guys know that I uh…I'm not going back to Bear Springs with you."

"What do you mean?" asked Harvey. "You're just a few days from your clearance."

Mick nodded. "I know. It's not about that." He reached behind him and pulled the FedEx packet from his waistband. "I've got some business up north that I need to take care of."

Harvey blinked with confusion. "Oh, I see." He reached for his wallet. "Well then. Do you need bus fare?"

Mick shook his head. "No thanks. There are some people here I gotta see before I go." Mick put out a hand. "Thank you, Harvey. For everything."

Harvey was in a state of shock. He reached out numbly and shook Mick's hand. "Be well, Mick."

It wasn't easy, but I managed to smile through my tears. When I tried to speak, my throat seized up. I opened my arms instead and gave him a silent goodbye. After our hug, Mick raised the envelope in the air and gave me a final nod. Then he turned and walked away.

Harvey called after him. "Mick? Is that all you've got?"

He looked over his shoulder with a crooked smile. "It's all I need."

As we watched him grow small in the distance, Stan, Piper, and Mom walked back to join us.

"What's Mick doing?" Mom asked, peering down the road.

I put my hands on my hips and gazed after him. "Following his heart."

When he finally slipped out of view, we turned and resumed our short stroll to the hotel. Harvey gestured toward

Stan and said, "Looks like you just got a cabin all to your-self—at least until we find Mick's replacement."

Across the parking lot, I spotted Colt with an enormous grin on his face as he tossed Wanda and Nicole's bags into the back of the pickup truck. The ladies were leaning against the truck, giggling like schoolgirls on the first day of summer. Their cheerful vibrance warmed my heart. We were all looking forward to getting back home.

Don't ask me why, but in my own surge of happiness, I suddenly flashed back to Nicole's amazing banana bread. "You know what, Harv? We don't need a new cook. We've already got a fantastic one right over there." I raised my eye-brows and pointed toward the other group. "What we need is a new waitress."

Harvey cocked his head. "Nicole? It never occurred to me. You think she'd want the job?"

"Mm-hmm. Especially if we give her a little creative license. I think she'd be thrilled."

Harvey's eyes brightened. "That's terrific! I'll let you give her the news."

Our group came to a stop just outside the hotel entrance. Harvey looked to Stan and asked, "What do you plan to do with your home, Stanley? Are you going to have it rebuilt?"

Stan shook his head. "I don't think so. I've kinda been thinking…it's time for a change."

"Oh?" Harvey answered. "Do you have a place in mind?"

Stan slipped an arm around my waist and smiled down at me. "Well, if it were up to me, I'd be putting down perma-nent roots…in the Bear Springs neighborhood."

The group fell silent.

"Stan?" My face flushed with uncertainty. "Are you…"

He let out a nervous laugh and shouted, "Yes, why not!" Then he grabbed my hands and said, "Pepper, I love you. Would you like to get married?"

❀ ❀ ❀

Stan took the dogs outside and made calls to the insurance company while Mom, Piper, and I packed our things. There was an odd energy in the room as we prepared to leave. I was still feeling woozy after Stan's impromptu proposal. Woozy, but elated. Mom was happy for me and probably a bit shocked. Piper was quiet, though. So I wasn't surprised when she looked up from her suitcase and said, "Hey, ladies?"

I backed out of the closet. "Yeah?"

"I think I'm gonna go home."

"You're going back to Scotty?" I asked.

She nodded. "We had a long talk last night. Scotty swore there was nothing more than the one hug between the two of them. But he admitted it was wrong and that he'd gotten off course." She shrugged her shoulders. "He apologized and…I realized I miss him. I really miss him."

"Aw, that's great, Pipe." I walked over and gave her a hug.

"Anyway, Bear Springs is way too much drama for me," she said with a tease.

I laughed, even though I was feeling her news like a punch in the gut. "Well, geez. You're not going home, too, are you, Mom?" Mom was at the end of her bed, folding and stacking clothes. The look on her face gave me pause. "Are you?" My stomach started to cramp as I watched her tilt her head this way and that, frowning in an inward debate.

"I wasn't supposed to say anything yet," she whined. Her worried eyes wandered toward me. "And I really hate to do it now. But being that this may be the last time I have you two in the same room, I suppose it's the right thing to do…" Piper and I looked at one another with apprehension. "Harvey and I have been making some plans," she began. "He's going to help me put the house on the market. And… we're getting married, too!" She pressed her lips together and widened her eyes, as though she might burst.

"Oh my goodness!" Piper and I raced to Mom and immersed her in a family hug. "I can't believe you two old-timers!" I exclaimed. "You have been holding out on us!"

Mom laughed and lowered her head in embarrassment. "Well, we're both out of practice at this sort of thing and… there was always so much going on."

"Wait a second," I said. "You knew about the family secret, didn't you?"

"Not until a few days ago. He decided he'd better tell me before things got too serious between us."

"Wow!" I shook my head. "So, you're going to live in his house in Fresno?"

"We'll be in Fresno; we'll be up at Bear Springs. We'll be wherever you need us, helping any way we can."

Piper climbed behind the wheel of her tow truck. I hoisted her last bag onto the passenger seat. "Gimme a call? Let me know you made it home safely?"

She nodded bravely. "And you don't be a stranger. I wanna know how things are going up there. And if you're ever in need of an undercover agent…" She smiled briefly.

Then her chin crumpled and a sob erupted from deep in her chest. "I love you, sis." Her bracelets jangled as she stretched her hand toward me.

I reached out and grasped her tight. "And I love you."

Harvey asked if I would like to lead us home, and I proudly assented. With Ranger by my side, I steered my old car into the pilot position and moved slowly, watching my rear like a mother duck, moving her babies across the pond for the first time. I couldn't help but smile when we reached the base of the mountain and began our upward climb, to the place where dreams were realized, and second chances were given. And where those you thought were gone forever, lived on.

www.ingramcontent.com/pod-product-compliance
Lightning Source LLC
Chambersburg PA
CBHW061244310726
48971CB00007B/2214